Hidden Things

An Ellen Parker Novel

Hidden Things

An Ellen Parker Novel

Steven M. Silver

Dedication

This one's for the bros: Mr. Hallan, Jay-Frog, and the Chairman.

Acknowledgements

Through my involvement with the Critical Incident Stress Debriefing programs in two Pennsylvania counties, requests for workshops and presentations to law enforcement agencies, and through my federal employment, I had the opportunity to meet with law enforcement officers at the local, county, state, and federal levels. With almost no exceptions, they all were competent professionals and good people. Some of the things they told me found their ways into the Ellen Parker series but I have not tried to write police procedurals, so my digressions from SOPs was my taking artistic license and not errors on their parts. I hope the various officers, deputies, troopers, and agents who shared their experiences with me enjoy these novels. The stories themselves are entirely works of fiction.

Alisti and Thub helped with editing and I am very, very grateful.

Part of the desire to get this story told came from the nagging of Lois Price – I kept putting it off, much to her frustration, but I finally bore down and got it done when I discovered she was examining unoccupied real estate featuring secluded pole barns in southern Pennsylvania. Read on…

Chester County, Pennsylvania
Summer, 2014

Day One

Chapter 1

The road the police officer rode went down a corn stalk corridor holding onto the August heat and humidity of eastern Pennsylvania. Above, dark clouds promised some kind of cooling rain. He glanced up through aviator sunglasses and wondered if the rain would, in fact, bring any cooling before it left – Pennsylvania, he knew, was an inveterate liar about its own weather.

He passed the marker for the Coalville borough limits but did not slow down; it was easier to turn his Ford Expedition around at the T-intersection a half mile ahead than wrestling the big SUV on the narrow road. That is why he saw the car with New York plates.

It was across and slightly down the crossing road as he stopped at the intersection. He turned and pulled in behind it, keeping the Expedition's right-hand wheels on pavement and angling its nose toward the road. The shoulder was narrow before giving way to a drainage ditch bordered by an old but still upright barbed wire fence.

The car was a recent and big Toyota SUV in white. He grinned; at least it wasn't in that silver that all Toyotas seemed to come in. Apparently, they did have another color.

It was barely off the road. He could see no one in it as he called its plate number into the dispatcher, feeling, not for the first time that day, a touch of irritation that his computer was still down. While waiting for his request for vehicle registration information, he flipped his flashers on. The officer picked up his dark blue cap from the seat and stepped out of the Ford.

He was a tall black man who had gotten into the habit, courtesy of the Pennsylvania Army National Guard and three tours in the sandbox, of shaving his head, though he permitted himself a carefully trimmed moustache. His clear brown eyes did nothing to hide the intelligence using them. His blue uniform shirt was short sleeved and revealed muscled arms his wife still insisted on describing, after twenty years, as "all business." On his chest, across from his silver Coalville police badge, a thin silver nametag bore the name "Peterson" and his collar tabs had small, silver sergeant chevrons.

It still looked like rain. A white man approached, walking across the field, burdened by a bag hanging over a shoulder and holding a camera. The dispatcher called back with no warrants or wants on the vehicle or its registered owner, a Robert Blasingame.

"I didn't get far enough off the road?" the man asked, pausing at the fence. He had sandy hair cut short and well, about two inches over six feet in height, weight around 190, though his shoulders beneath an old plaid felt shirt suggested he might be closer to 200, blue jeans, and ankle-high gray hiking shoes. He had smile lines and pale blue eyes that drooped at the ends, a curious combination of humor and sadness coexisting on his face.

"You're good," Peterson said. He stepped across the ditch. "May I see your license, sir?"

"Sure," Blasingame said. He opened his bag and put his camera into it and then produced his wallet. He handed over his license. It had a better than average picture of him and his name.

"Thank you, Mister Blasingame," Peterson said. He handed the license back. "What were you taking pictures of, the crash site?"

"Not really," Blasingame said. He looked back across the field. "I'm an amateur photographer and I wanted to try to get some shots of the plant life coming back." He pointed. "The burned area goes into the trees bordering the field and you can see where bushes and things got crushed by the impact." He turned back to the officer and smiled slightly. "It's the contrast that I was trying for, the flattened stuff and the new sprouts, the black area and the new green. Not some kind of ghoul, just like to take pictures of nature. For a photography class I'm taking."

"What kind of camera are you using?"

Blasingame opened the lid of the bag and took out a black camera.

"It's a Canon EOS. I really need to take a class in operating it. The thing is smarter than I am." He grinned.

He said it with the kind of self-deprecating tone men use when they don't want to brag but are probably pretty proficient at whatever skill they are talking about. Peterson nodded.

"Can I see some of your work?"

"Sure." Blasingame took a second to bring the display to life and then he handed the camera to Peterson. "That's the last shot. You can scroll back by… You got it. Probably know more about these things than I do."

"Not likely," Peterson said as he looked at the pictures. "My car's computer has taken a personal affront to me and I haven't been able to get anything but a big blue error message all shift. I'd shoot the damned thing but then there would be all that paperwork."

Blasingame chuckled and then tilted his neck to see the screen.

"I think that's the best of them."

"It is a good shot," Peterson said, nodding. "You have an eye for photos."

"Thanks." He turned and looked back at the burned field.

"I don't really know much about what happened, just caught it on the news last month."

"Yeah, the fire spread fast," Peterson said. There were no more pictures to see and he handed the camera back to Blasingame. "It was pretty dry and had been for a while. Our fire people had their hands full beating it down."

"The news talked a lot about the townspeople pitching in," Blasingame said as he put the camera in its bag and checked the lid's latches. He rested his hands on the top wire. "Volunteers."

"Small town, everyone knows everyone; trouble comes, people pitch in to help. We're not like the bigger towns like Downingtown south of here where you only know the people living next door."

"Were you here?"

"Not immediately," Peterson said. "I'd just gotten off night shift when I got the recall. By the time I arrived, you had the whole fire department here. They came through a gate over there," he pointed down the road, "and were working on both the wreck and the trees."

"Were the volunteers already here?"

"Most of them," Peterson said, "though people kept arriving all through the morning." He shook his head. "Bad stuff. The place was a mess. The plane actually hit at first in the field beyond the gate, kind of bounced through the fence over there and tumbled. The fire, well, you can see where it really flared up. That was the forward portions of the plane, where the engines came to rest." He shook his head again. "Bad stuff. All thirty-two people died in the crash."

"Twenty-seven in the crash," Blasingame said. "Five on the way to or in the hospital."

You don't know much about it but you know where they all died.

Peterson nodded, saying nothing, but a small alarm bell went off in the part of his brain that was Coalville Township Police Department blue.

"Well, Mister Blasingame," he said, "this is private land and…"

"I understand," Blasingame said. He took off his bag and reached over the fence to put it on the ground but the officer held out his hand. Blasingame grinned. "Thanks."

Blasingame put both hands on the top of the post and, with little seeming effort, vaulted over the fence. Peterson handed him the bag.

"Thanks again, sergeant," Blasingame said, slipping the strap over his shoulder.

"No problem," Peterson said. "Where are you headed?"

"Here, actually. On vacation. I want to spend some time taking pictures of barns and covered bridges, and I really want to see some of the antique stores. Thought I'd slip over to Lancaster County for the Amish farms."

"Good place for it," Peterson said. "Just don't take pictures of the Amish themselves. They dislike it."

"Gotcha."

"Staying at the motel?"

"No, I've got reservations at the Willow Run Bed and Breakfast. Have you heard anything about it?"

"I'm told it's pretty good," Peterson said. "Newer place, been in business just a few years. Nice ladies run it. It's just a mile west of here."

"My first time here. And my first vacation in a couple of years." He smiled again. "Motels seem too much like business, you know? So, I figured a B and B would be nicer."

"They seem to be making a go of it," Peterson said. "Near Willow Run, you have a couple of fast food places but, if you go looking for dinner, there's a nice restaurant right in the center of town. Alfredo's. And a diner next to the township buildings, it's pretty good." He smiled slightly. "It's where most of the police go."

"Thanks for the information," Blasingame said. He held out his hand. "Be safe, sergeant."

"Thanks," Peterson said, shaking his hand. "I'll wait until you've pulled out."

Peterson waited in his car, its blue and reds flashing, as Blasingame drove onto the road and then turned around at the gate. As he came back, Peterson raised his hand to Blasingame's wave. Then he picked up his microphone.

"Dispatch, Peterson. Run a check for me on a Robert L. Blasingame, address on his vehicle registration that you just ran."

4

Hidden Things

Copy, Sergeant Peterson.
The alarm bell was still insisting, though very gently, that attention be paid to it.

Ellen Parker drove her Honda CR-V through Coalville, a journey that took relatively little time as the town was small, almost tiny. Well, it was, at least in comparison, if you worked in Philadelphia.

She silently offered the town an apology. Back in Ohio, where she grew up, small towns were the rule – getting down to Cincinnati was a big deal.

Now here I am, all jaded, so much so that I use words like 'jaded.'

She smiled, something she did easily. A thin woman, what in southern Ohio might have been called "rawboned" with only slight exaggeration, her high cheekbones and sharp nose were softened by brown eyes that looked around her with openness.

Ellen slowed down at a pedestrian crossing in the middle of a block as a woman and child stepped onto it. The woman looked in her direction and nodded as Ellen stopped. Ellen looked around while she waited.

Coalville was dominated by one- and two-story buildings. All seemed in good shape with none needing paint. Bright banners hung from lampposts; some said "PA's heart!" while others "Welcome Home!"

The crosswalk clear, she let her car roll forward. The Garmin told her to look for an upcoming right hand turn off of Stanford Avenue, which the county road bringing her into town had magically turned into. She came up on the cross street and made her right. Very quickly, she was out of town and surrounded by country. Small town, indeed.

Five minutes later, the Garmin insisted she was at her destination, which appeared to be a single, gravel-covered lane. She turned onto it and ignored the Garmin's insistence she turn around. The lane took her through some trees and then, when the county road behind her disappeared, she arrived at a paved parking lot and scattered buildings, all dominated by a two-story log cabin.

A carved sign out front said, "Willow Run B&B". She smiled and stretched before opening the door.

Now her vacation officially started.

Ellen swung the car door wide and stepped out of the car. While the parking lot pavement reflected the heat, the woods were close to the buildings, almost cradling them, and she looked forward to walking through the trees.

"Are you Ellen Parker?" a woman's voice called from within the log cabin.

"I am," she said. "I'm early." She looked but could see no one behind the screen door.

"Not a problem," the woman said. "Come on in."

Ellen walked into the cabin and found herself in a broad room with heavily padded chairs and couches. To the left a closed door stood beside a staircase that disappeared above. Paintings of wildlife competed with photographs of country scenes – both appeared to be done by good artists – and both covered the walls above waist-high bookshelves. The shelves were full of paperbacks and hardbound books. Board games piled on a shelf threatened to collapse into themselves and Ellen wondered how Monopoly and Scrabble would merge. Maybe spell your way out of jail?

To the right, the room opened on a dining area almost as large. Small tables with pairs of chairs stood against the walls while a long table, big enough to encourage wondering how it had managed to be brought in, took up the middle with a dozen chairs, only three of which matched.

"Back in here," the voice said from beyond the dining room and Ellen walked further into the house.

She found the woman in the kitchen putting away blue dishes. While the kitchen had a well-lit island, it seemed, after the first two rooms, surprisingly small.

The woman was tall and broad shouldered with a white person's complexion reflecting a fair amount of time spent outdoors. Ellen recognized her from the web site where she made her reservations; her name was Patti Taylor and she was, the site said, "Primary Cook, kitchen Czarina, and struggling Gardner." Though in her mid-40s, something she did not attempt to camouflage, she looked like athletics were still a part of her life.

"Pour yourself some coffee," Patti said. "Behind you, it's set up for use any time."

Ellen turned and found a coffee urn with a bunch of cups, all different, all handmade, spread across a broad shelf above it. She poured herself a cup.

"Cream, real thing, in the fridge," Pattie said taking bowls from the dishwasher.

"Prefer it straight," Ellen said. "Can I pour you one?"

"Thanks," Patti said, "but I'm still working on one somewhere around here. Switch to tea for dinner." She looked up. "You read all the stuff on the site?"

"Pretty much," Ellen said.

Patti faced her, a smile appearing as she found her coffee cup. She took a sip.

"Breakfast starts at seven, done by nine, in the evening we put out cheese, wine, fruit, that sort of thing. Food bars and fruit always in the fridge, use them any time. Books, borrow whatever you like, drop off any of your own you don't want to carry home."

"Who's your photographer?"

"Like those? They're by our guests. We had several birders who took a zillion pictures and sent some back to us. And the deer ones, they're by a professional fella whose stuff is in Sports Illustrated. He got tired of taking pictures of concussions, I guess. He's in Australia now, documenting what they're doing after their wildfires."

"They're pretty good."

"You a photographer?"

"No," Ellen said. "I've worked with some and I like to get outdoors."

"You know from our site that we're surrounded by trees. State game land just to the west, county park to the south, numerous trails all round, there's a map in your room. Please use it because we try not to give the search and rescue people any more business than we have to."

Ellen nodded.

"You're here for the week," Patti said. "So we have you in the furthest cabin from here, which we call the 'main house' because we are bereft of imagination. We have a fellow from New York staying a week and a couple of guys staying a week, but everyone else is one- or two-night people. One family coming in tonight. Lots of kids. Regulars, this is their third visit. They'll be upstairs here in the main house. Shouldn't be too rowdy."

"I'll try not to be myself."

"Too bad. Anyway, Joyce will do breakfast tomorrow morning. Watch out for her; her goal in life is to make a piece of French toast large enough to sink a good-sized container ship."

"I think I'm in love."

"Sorry, she's taken. We've got WI-FI via cable; cellphone service here can be spotty. Landline phone here in the kitchen with our number and all the usual emergency numbers on the posted sheet beside it. We live back up the lane near the entrance and can get here pretty quick if you need us."

"Laundry? The site didn't say."

"Carefully guarded secret. Utility room out the back door, beyond the dining room, on the right. If you use it, wait until after everyone in the main house has done their morning showers as it draws on the same hot water tank. Not a problem if you are using just cold water. Early afternoon is usually safe. If you are in a rush, there's a coin-op in town, just as you enter from here. Look to the right, right after the golden arches but before the Wise Owl book store."

"Thanks." Ellen paused. "Anything besides deer in the woods?"

"Occasional dragons, that sort of thing," Patti said, "but not this time of year."

"Already migrated east, then, have they?"

"Pretty much. We have coyotes, you'll probably never see them."

"Why not?"

"Maybe a Navy SEAL, bless their black hearts, could get close enough, but most people are too noisy in the trees. Skunks, raccoons, you want to keep your distance because of the possibility of rabies. County has stopped counting rabid animals. If they approach you, that's usually a pretty good signal to back off."

"All right."

"Anything else I can tell you? I'll make things up if I don't know the answer."

"Sounds like some of the people I've interviewed. No, no other questions."

"Let's get your key and let me show you your cabin."

The cabin was larger than Ellen expected. Two queen-sized beds, covered by quilted blankets, dominated the pine-paneled room but it had a pair of well-padded chairs facing a wide picture window. A solid table with a firmer chair was against a wall with a small card describing the log-on procedures for the WI-FI connection. A chest of drawers bordered a wall. A large bathroom was in the back.

"Very nice," she said and Patti grinned.

"Be sure to leave your porch light on," Patti said. "You're facing away from the main house and night around here gets very dark."

"That's all right," Ellen said. "I kind of like the night."

"Some people do."

"I think we'll take that service plaza," the driver of the dark blue Chevy Suburban said as the green sign with white lettering came into view; the sun was going down behind it and it was hard to see clearly in spite of his sunglasses. He was white and in his late forties. He wore his hair short along his temples that partially hid his scattering of gray hair and made him look like he had been a soldier at some time, an occupation he had never tried. Like the man next to him, he wore a sport coat. Both men wore tinted aviator-style sunglasses but only the driver sported a tie. People who knew of him, and there were very few who did, just knew him as Radisson, no first name. Only a very few knew his first name was Daniel, only one person on Earth was allowed to call him Danny, and that person sat next to him. "How far to our exit?"

"Morgantown exit is about eight miles from here, six from the service center. There should be a motel right after the exit. Or we can press on to Coalville."

"I want to come on it in the morning. Did you do that math in your head?" He liked to tease his partner.

His partner was a few years younger, more athletic appearing, and wore his hair short in imitation of Radisson, though his was obviously a reddish blond. His name was Michael Bornstein. People who knew him had, when he was much younger, called him Mikey. Since he had teamed up with Radisson, anyone who knew him just called him by his last name. The two men had been lovers for four years.

"Had to use my fingers. Quick trip from Allentown. Less than an hour."

"We spent that long trying to get our lunch there. Worst airport I've ever flown into."

"Did you hear what Graber said about it?"

"That it sucked?"

"He's a pilot, he ought to know. On the other hand, using our own plane made it easier to get our stuff in and out past security."

"He used to be a smuggler. Goes back to the cowboy days. Knows all the tricks."

"I think I could teach him a couple."

"Don't pick on the straight people, Michael. It's cruel."

"Car guys were on top of things, though."

"Always nice to use a car with local plates. I don't like standing out."

"Have you seen this boat?"

"Which one?"

9

"The one by Hinckley. This one." He held up the magazine from his lap and Radisson took a quick look. "Matt Lauer has one."

"Yeah, the *Picnic*. Very nice."

"They do good work, but it's pricey."

"Well, yeah, Matt Lauer. Television guy, he's got to have a fortune."

"But we can dream."

"Always. I don't suppose Mr. Fredericks' friend down in Florida handles Hinckleys."

"Already checked the brochure. Afraid not."

"I like the Whaler 360 more, anyway."

"You just like three outboards."

"I am an outboard man, no question. You want to call Mr. Books, let him know we're about to enter his territory? Tell him where we're going to spend the night, so he understands we're not pressing in without telling him."

"Always pays to be courteous. I'll call his guy when we stop at the plaza."

"And let Mr. Fredericks know we tipped our hat politely to Mr. Books. He'll want to know that we didn't forget."

"All in the nature of political politeness."

Radisson chuckled as he hit his turn signal.

"Mr. Books probably is worried," he said as he negotiated the ramp into the plaza, "that we're going to start shooting up the place like Wyatt Earp, being from New York and all."

"We're not?" Bornstein took off his sunglasses and revealed gray-blue eyes. "You never let me have any fun."

"Keep thinking about that 360," Radisson said, grinning at the other man's joke and revealing smile lines deeply creasing his face. "We'll have a hell of a lot of fun with that."

"Not only with that," the other man said, stroking the inside of Radisson's thigh as they pulled into a parking place. He smiled and opened the door. "Got to make my call," he said and stepped out.

"Teaser," Radisson said. "I'm going to hit the rest room. You want a soda?"

"No cruising," the other man said, raising his smart phone and studying the screen. "Yes, please, whatever diet they have."

"Got it." He turned to go.

"You're snagged," Bornstein said, his voice low, and Radisson stopped.

Keeping his back to his car door, Radisson felt behind him and freed his coat from the handgun he carried. The Suburban was tall and the door was a good shield.

"Thanks," he said. He adjusted his coat. "All right now?"

"You're fine."

"Didn't even think to check," Radisson said. He shook his head. "Good thing we're retiring."

"Hey, on the road all day. Get tired, distracted."

"No excuse," Radisson said, his voice firm. "Be right back."

Bornstein watched him go and then punched a number into his phone. There was no question that Radisson was a professional, but sometimes he was too hard on himself. No slack at all.

Of course, in their business, which had nothing to do with fishing boats and everything to do with the Glocks both men carried, slack was for amateurs.

Day Two

Chapter 2

It was an effort – after all, this was a vacation – but Ellen Parker was out of her bed with the sunrise. She thought it was the most continuous sleep she had gotten in a year and wondered if she could find out the name of the mattress.

Or maybe another job. The news business took over a person's waking hours and then required that one's life become all "waking hours." That was her theory and, judging from her own experience and that of her colleagues, it was valid.

Though tempted, she left her cell phone off and took a small sense of satisfaction that this was the second day without using it. A record.

She was the kind of person who was serious about her workouts. They were not a vehicle for anything else and her dress reflected her approach. Her shorts were rotated from various Philadelphia universities' stores and were selected for durability and ease of motion rather than how well they displayed her butt. Old sweatshirts, including a red and gold Marine Corps one from a friend she had nearly died beside, served as tops. A bandanna, this one was blue, served as a sweatband. Her sports bra was snug and selected for comfort. Being small-chested, she sometimes wore one under her street clothes. Only her running shoes, Asics, were a national brand and she wore them without socks.

Ellen stretched briefly and then, her wristwatch serving as a timer, went down on the dewy grass and did push-ups, picking up the speed of her repetitions. She hated push-ups, always did them and never cheated, keeping her body perfectly level with each one. That her personality was reflected in each repetition was not something she would have noticed but might have conceded.

Ellen did not exercise for appearance but, and this she knew, for survival. She had been close to death within the past year and once before. One part of her way of responding to the trauma was to do everything she could to ensure she was as strong as she needed to be.

13

A star-shaped scar marred her right thigh; it still felt odd, like it was numb, and stiff, and a little itchy, all three at once, and the doctor experienced with gunshot wounds – she checked his bio through her newspaper employer and found he volunteered for several tours with the Guard in Iraq and Afghanistan – said the itchiness would fade, the stiffness would respond to rehab, and the numbing in the center of the wound would likely persist. She did all the rehab they prescribed and then added to it by picking up her running routine.

Ellen ran the occasional 5Ks and liked the cardio, but she did not share the real reason she ran – control. She found satisfaction in the discipline of running, pushing herself to get better, overcoming the temptation to pull back, to quit.

She jogged past the other cabins until she reached the parking area and then picked up her pace. The road was still covered by shadow and the sun was in her eyes, so she was a little cautious about how hard she pushed herself.

She was almost to the highway when she saw a man running in front of her. He had the easy stride of someone who was accustomed to running and she envied his grace; her own style she referred to as "getting it done" and thought there was nothing about how she did it that was anything other than utilitarian.

She caught up to him at the road, nodded, and turned back toward the cabins. The man, a taller white man running bare-chested, his t-shirt held in one hand, nodded back, said "Good morning," but nothing else as he turned and followed.

Ellen did several laps on the road and she and the man smiled at one another each time they passed. But when she did her last lap back to the cabins, she did not encounter him and felt vaguely disappointed.

She showered and resisted the temptation to turn on her laptop to check the news, email from work, or anything else. This was supposed to be a vacation, she reminded herself. The cell phone remained off and she began to count up the hours it had been silent before gently chastising herself and dropping it into the bottom of her handbag.

She dressed in jeans and Salomon's Discovery GTX hiking shoes, planning on spending some time on the forest trails. From her collection and suspecting the day would be cool, she picked a sweatshirt from a drawer. Also from a friend who had learned of her collection, it was a hooded gray one with a small FBI logo over the heart. Her friend, an FBI agent wounded in the same case

Ellen was, assured her it wasn't official but, "It looks better than the ones sold to tourists."

Ellen stepped outside and saw the day was promising to be a good one with some of the heat and humidity lifting. Pushing back the sleeves of her sweatshirt, she made her way to the main house.

The dining room was nearly full. A family with several children occupied the large, central table and seemed to be having some kind of contest involving giggling; the parents appeared to have abandoned their roles as referees and had become contestants. Two couples of young men were at other tables. The runner from the morning was at a small table with a book – a real book, even though it was a paperback – and holding a large cup of coffee in one hand while his eyes were on her. Though smiling, his eyebrows went up. Ellen took one of the remaining tables, one near his. Patti was by her table almost immediately.

"Coffee and tea in the usual place," she said. "We've got fresh orange and apple juice and some cranberry. Waffles and pancakes and Joyce is making killer omelets to order. Oh, and the waffles are stuffed with blueberries. The kids," she nodded towards the children at the central table, "seem to have endorsed them."

"I'll try one," Ellen said.

"How about an omelet? The spinach is fresh but you can have just about anything you can imagine."

"All right, how about spinach, mushrooms, and mixed cheese?"

"Hardly a challenge – Joyce may feel insulted." Patti grinned. "Lawyers get like that. Maybe she'll sue. Juice is on the counter."

The mention of her name had Joyce come to the edge of the dining area, wiping her hands with a hand towel. She was shorter and younger than Patti and had a large smile on her square face.

"Omelet on the way," she said. "Let me know what you think of the mushrooms. They're from Kennett Square, just down the road. And Patti is right, I do like a challenge."

"I know Kennett," Ellen said, "and I'll try and do better tomorrow."

"Good girl." Patti went off to the kitchen with Joyce and Ellen looked around and met the runner's eyes. He was still smiling and she returned one.

"FBI?" he asked, his eyebrows up which seemed to emphasize the sad droop of his eyes.

15

"Gift from a friend," she said. The kids laughed, though at what, Ellen did not know.

"Oh, good," he said, still smiling. The eyebrows came down. "Glad to see I'm not being arrested."

"Maybe later."

"Bob Blasingame," he said, holding out his hand. Ellen hesitated for a heartbeat and then took his hand. He shook firmly but did not try to impress her with his strength by crushing her hand.

"Ellen Parker," she said. As they released hands, she nodded at the book. "What are you reading?"

He held up the book. It was a guide for a type of Canon camera.

"Are you a photographer?" she asked as she stood and walked to the juice.

"Strictly amateur," he said. "I'm taking classes, adult education thing, at my local community college." He waited until she returned and sat down. "I've always been interested in photography but finally decided to get some instruction on it."

"It's a real art," Ellen said. "I know some pros. What do you do in real life?" Her question got a broad grin.

"In real life…" he said, the grin continuing. "I work in construction. Mostly nowadays, supplying contractors working on old houses and buildings. Restoration projects. Lot of time on the road, looking for things like facades, leaded glass, brass work, all that kind of thing. And you?"

"I work for the Philadelphia Enquirer, on the online side."

"A reporter?" The eyebrows went back up.

"That and some assistance on the editorial desk."

"You may be the person I'm looking for," Blasingame said, still smiling. "Oh?"

"Well, sort of. I'm on vacation and all but my homework assignment from class is developing a photo project, so I'm doing some work on it. Yesterday, I was at the plane crash site, you know, the one north of here." The smile had faded.

"I know it," she said.

"Of course. Reporter. Anyway, I'm planning on getting some pictures of old buildings and barns but I got the idea of documenting how the fields at the crash site are coming back. The vegetation, I mean. Growth and all that. I got, I think, some good pictures yesterday. What I'd like to do is see if there are any pictures from the day of the crash itself of the field or maybe in the days that followed that I can use as kind of a 'Before' statement."

"Ah, and you are wondering what the newspaper might have?"

"Well, actually, that would be great, but what I was thinking was you might be able to tell me what the local newspaper is and who I might talk to about seeing their back issues."

"I saw most of what went to the public. The local newspaper is the Daily Local. They're county-wide. You can go back through their website and see what they had. We used imagery from a number of local individuals as well as the usual feeds and links. But what you see in back issues or online is going to be maybe five percent of what they actually have. Most of the pictures immediately available are going to be the usual. Shots of the plane, shots of the rescue and fire workers, that kind of thing. If someone paused to take pictures of the burning or destroyed foliage, it probably wasn't used and is in the archives."

"How does someone get into the archives?"

"Depending on the source, they may charge a fee or have a protocol restriction based on how recent the material is." Ellen looked up as Patti appeared with a large platter of omelet and blue-flecked waffle.

"Let me know what you think," Patti said and then was gone again. The family trooped out and one of the couples followed closely.

"It may be a bad idea," Blasingame said, sipping at his coffee.

"I think it might be an interesting contrast," Ellen said. The omelet was delicious.

"Are you on vacation, too?"

"Yes," she said, nodding. "But I don't have a homework assignment. I'm just really looking to kick back and take it easy."

"Good area for it," he said, wiping his mouth. "Nice little town. Some of their buildings are from the early Nineteenth Century, part of the growth spurt they had when the steel mills really hit high gear here in Pennsylvania. There are a few that are even older that have managed to survive. I'm hoping to check out some of them." He stood up. "How long are you here?"

"A week," she said. "You?"

"It's a little open-ended, but it might be a week." He hesitated and seemed to be studying her face. Finally, he smiled. "Maybe I'll see you later."

"It's a nice town," Ellen said. She found herself wanting to say more but all she came up with, "Enjoy yourself."

Blasingame left. Her eyes followed and she noticed that the remaining male couple also watched him leave. After he was gone, one man leaned over to another and whispered something to his partner, who grinned, rubbed his goatee, and whispered something back that got a short laugh. She returned to her food.

Ellen finished breakfast and spent some time on the porch before embarking on her hike in the forest. The two young men came outside, smiled and nodded at her, and got into a Subaru with a rainbow decal on the back. She watched them drive away.

So, girl, what are you thinking? Maybe pushing your vacation into something more?

Ellen remembered Blasingame's bare chest as she jogged past and smiled slightly to herself. It was a nice chest but the shoulders…

I am a shoulder and butt slut.

She nodded as she stepped off the porch; things were better since last year, since the violence, since the deaths. Boundaries, lines she had not felt she could cross, had shifted since all that. So maybe it was time to do a little… pushing. Ellen grinned, faintly mocking herself and turned toward the trees.

Blasingame drove into Coalville and found an unmetered spot on a street off the main square. He slung his camera on a shoulder while he opened his smart phone. He paused, checking messages. There was one that he nodded at before deleting. He moved his thumb and called up a list of street addresses, each with a brief note, of places in Coalville. Another thumb bounce and he studied a map of the town. Blue dots on it matched the list and he was pleased to see one was just down the street from him.

It was a building that once held offices but now was simply a place of storage. He walked around the single-story structure and took pictures. Constructed of stone, something they seemed have plenty of in Pennsylvania, it looked a little like a castle. He was mostly interested in the doors, several of which appeared to be as old as the stone walls.

Blasingame took pictures of the doors' hardware and studied the display of the shots and finally nodded. He did not consult his list or the GPS-aided map but turned and walked towards the square. A minute later, he entered an antique store, one he had identified before coming to Coalville.

"Good morning," an older woman said from behind a glass counter that looked like it was cleaned every day. Tables and shelves, all in neat rows, held antiques of various kinds; the little of the room's walls that could be seen suggested the room was older than some of its antiques.

"Morning," Blasingame said. "My name's Bob Blasingame. I'm down from New York. I look for items for contractors restoring historic homes. I saw on your website you handle such things."

"Yes, we do," she said. She held out her hand and he took it. "I'm Clara Delaney. I do the clerking, my husband does the gathering. He's on the road today, going to an auction near Lancaster, but I can give you the grand tour."

"Great. I'm interested in everything but a couple of my clients are looking for some large doors and their hardware."

"Well, let's see," she said. "Our bigger things are out back and I know we do have some doors. You mean like front doors, solid, maybe with some ornamentation?"

"Yes."

"I think we have a few of those. Let's go look."

Blasingame smiled broadly and followed the older woman. But, once they were in the large storeroom, the doors turned out to be too narrow.

"Well, that's too bad," Clara said. She did not appear to be too bothered by the lack of a sale. "You can always trim them back but you can't make them larger."

"Not without a lot of work," Blasingame said. "But I saw some brass items when we came in. I'd like to take a look at them."

The items were hardware for windows and he bought all they had of a particular style. She ran his credit card, he made small talk.

"You all had that terrible plane crash last month," he said.

"Yes, we did. Frightful." She handed him the slip and he signed.

"I saw some of it on the news. It looked like a lot of people from town pitched in to help out."

"Yes, they did. It wasn't all that far from town."

"Were you there?"

"With the fire police. My husband is on their squad and I and some of the others, we run sort of a coffee truck. While he was helping to direct traffic, we passed out cups of coffee and such for the firefighters."

"Nice. Who got there first? Someone told me that some people got there ahead of the fire department."

"Well, a few did," she said. "But most people got there at the same time or after. It did take them a little while to get the trucks and ambulance out there."

"Of course."

"I think the very first people were the Johnston brothers, because their garage is on the side of town closest to the crash. Anyway, that's what I was told. There was a small group up where the fuselage came to a halt while the firefighters worked on the fire further back."

"I saw that the fire got into the trees."

"Yes, the north side of the field. We haven't had a lot of rain, so the fire moved there. From the wings."

"One of your police officers, a sergeant, pointed that out to me."

"The cockpit section was to one side," she said. She seemed to need to talk and Blasingame said nothing. "It was all collapsed and everything. The fuselage had tumbled and rolled. It was hard to tell what it was. They found some people who were still alive but they were pretty bad off. The EMTs tried very hard but none of them made it."

"Did the Johnston brothers find the five?"

"I don't think they did. Those five were in a back section, people said. I don't know, really, who found them. The Johnstons... I'm not sure. I heard they were about the first to get there. Marilyn Richards, her husband is the Assistant Chief, said they put out a small fire using their own extinguishers."

"Not in the wings."

"Oh, no, not the wings. Those fires, well, they were pretty big. They were the source of the fire that tried to get into the trees. Not the wings."

"There was other fire?"

"Yes, yes there was. Around the biggest part of the fuselage. Not the tail section where they found those five poor people but the part that was down the field."

"Good they were able to help."

"Yes, it was." She smiled. "You know, when things get bad, sometimes people really surprise you."

"That's true."

"Let me get you a cardboard box for those latches. I think they'll tear through the bags I have."

"Thank you."

Blasingame waited as Clara went behind another counter and finally emerged with a solid cardboard box. It turned out to be just the right size.

"I appreciate you taking the time to show me those doors."

"Happy to," she said. She reached under the counter and came back with a card she handed to him. "If there's anything else you find yourself needing, let us know. That's got our email address. There are always things popping up and we can keep an eye out for you."

"I certainly will," Blasingame said, studying the card. He turned to leave.

"Have a good day," she said.

"You, too."

Blasingame stored the box in the back of his SUV and arranged an old blanket around it to keep it from sliding around. He took out his phone and tapped the display.

There were a lot of antique stores in Coalville and he planned to hit them all as well as several older buildings he wanted to see.

And people to talk to.

Radisson looked over at Bornstein as he slid into his seat.

"Off the street?" he asked and Bornstein nodded.

"Ground floor. Number thirty-one. And, as per their website, all rooms have safes. Swing around to the left and that takes us to the back. She said the pool's back there."

"I could use a swim," Radisson said as he slowly drove the car through the motel's entrance. "I used to do a lot of swimming."

"Everyone says it's good for you. I like it."

"You're too dedicated to it for me," Radisson said. He bent his neck to look around the edge of the building and continued forward. "You go to the Y every day. It's like a job."

"Naw, not really. It clears my head. Good start for the day. You ought to try it. I mean, you like swimming."

"I do but daily laps…" He shook his head. "Like a job."

"Hey, it gives me that figure you like."

"I do, I do. Here we are." He shut the car down. "We got anything?"

Bornstein pulled out his phone and tapped the screen.

"One message." He tapped. "Nothing. Just letting us know Mr. Fredericks talked with Mr. Johns. The pick-up lady is back in position at Harrisburg and our guy is here in Coalville. We're still good to go."

"Anyone seen anything?"

"No mention of it, so I assume not. They'd say if there was any sign of it."

"Oh, yeah, they would. Let's unpack and try out the pool."

21

"Got to be better than that place last night," Bornstein said as he climbed out of the car.

"Too close to the turnpike, too much traffic," Radisson said. He got out and walked back to the rear of the SUV. He paused to stretch. "I had trouble sleeping."

"Noticed you tossing and turning."

"Hope I didn't keep you up."

"No. You know me. I can sleep through just about anything."

"Great talent – wish I had it."

"Maybe," Bornstein said, smiling as he raised the hatch, "it's because I swim laps every day."

"You are a natural born trouble maker."

"Yep, I sure am." He reached in and took out a rolling suitcase and a small cooler. "Natural born."

Radisson took out his bag. He dropped the hatch and then made sure it was locked.

They entered the building and turned into the hall that took them to their room. They used the room safe to store their Glocks, unpacked and changed into swim trunks. A few minutes later they returned to the pool and put the cooler between their lounge chairs.

"Nice morning," Radisson said.

"Messages," Bornstein said, lifting his phone from a towel. He tapped it and raised an eyebrow. "Some good news from Fredericks' guy in Albany. He says Philly said they have nothing. Nothing has shown up anywhere, nothing all the way down to Miami, all the way to Chicago. Zip."

"I think Fredericks would call that bad news."

"Well, it may still be *here* is the point he was making."

"What's the other message?"

"From our boy."

"That's quick."

"He's supposed to be pretty good."

"He is. What's the message?"

"He may have a lead. Wants to check something out but we may have a customer."

"Good. Tell him we're ready to go."

"Ok. Anything else?"

"He prefers brevity. That's enough." Radisson reached into the cooler and pulled out a diet cola – he was watching his weight.

"On the way." Bornstein put his phone back on the towel. "Brevity?"

"No nonsense guy. Worked with him years ago. Doesn't mess around. When I heard Fredericks sent him, I was surprised we got the nod to work with him."

"Usually takes care of business himself?"

"Absolutely." He nodded as he took a sip. "Fredericks uses him for things that have to be dealt with quickly. Significant things. Remember Domingo?"

"That was him?"

"All by himself."

"Shit." Bornstein reached down and took a beer from the cooler. "I see why you wondered why we got tapped."

Radisson shrugged.

"Fredericks doesn't take chances. From how he talked, with so many unknowns, he might be thinking our guy may be walking into a lions' den and wanted some additional firepower around." He shrugged as he took a sip. "You know, we're sort of invited guests of Mr. Books but sometimes that business networking falls apart."

"We're not just here for the Q and A?"

"I think that's all we'll do, but, yes, playing it safe. A little back-up."

"I understand."

"I'm not worried. Neither of us are cherries and our guy is pretty sharp. If it is O.K. Corral time, he'll stack the odds in our favor. He knows what he is doing. Besides, Fredericks is being very careful to keep Books in the loop."

"I feel all reassured and everything." Bornstein stood up. "Just remind me again how big a payday this is and that we're retiring after it's over."

"It's huge and we are. And we'll talk more about the possible opportunity I mentioned on the ride down."

"Coolio. Remember, we need to find a place to work." He turned and took several steps to the edge of the pool. He dived in smoothly and Radisson remembered that Bornstein had swum for his college team a couple of decades ago.

It would be fine, he told himself. Probably all they would do was some of the 'Q and A' Bornstein referred to. But if anything else needed doing, they could handle it. They always had.

And if an interesting opportunity opened up, well, they might, after all, get a Hinckley like Matt Lauer's.

Joyce, her hands absent-mindedly drying themselves on a kitchen towel, leaned against a porch post and watched Ellen Parker disappear into the forest.

Though the younger woman had not tried to advertise it, Joyce knew she was a journalist. More, thanks to Patti's interest in "women's affairs," an opportunity for double-entendre if there ever was one, she knew Ellen was the person who wrote an excellent article on women veterans of Iraq and Afghanistan a couple of years ago.

And more.

It was Ellen Parker, along with a pair of those women vets, who did in the self-styled "Dr. John," a sadistic serial killer. Joyce was impressed with her courage – yes, for her suicidal lunge at the man that gave the other two women a chance to put that bastard face down in a forest clearing, but, more than that, for her ability to write about what happened in that dark night and what he had done to her.

It had all happened not far from here. Was that the reason she had chosen Willow? Testing the healing?

Joyce nodded; Ellen may have helped other women by her willingness to openly tell her story. Maybe helped herself, too.

She carefully folded the towel. Now that woman was walking off into a forest alone. Joyce nodded for a second time. The Parker girl, she decided as she turned to walk back indoors, was alright.

"That's what it is, a clearing on a hillside just off a hiking trail," Ellen said aloud. Nearby, a singing bird, interrupted, went silent. She stepped further into the clearing.

It was very much like the Other One. Of course, the Other One she first saw in the night, after being assaulted, escaping and running for her life only to be re-captured. Not caring very much about her own life, she had tried to throw herself at the killer so the others could run away. He shot her and was killed by the others; it had not occurred to them to use her distraction to run away. It had not occurred to them leave any of their own behind and that included her.

This was a bright day, no one was chasing her, and no one wanted her dead. Yes, it was a clearing. Similar in appearance. And that was all. The therapy hours had worked, though she had been pressured into getting the help by the two friends from that clearing, the Other One, with her. They would be glad to know it worked, though she already told them with gratitude it had.

Ellen walked through it, enjoying the warmth of direct sunlight after the morning cool of the forest shadows. As clearings went, she decided, it was a good one.

She found herself, from time to time, testing herself, exploring to see what remained of her trauma. She likened it to exploring an extracted tooth with your tongue, seeing if any pain remained.

But there was none. It was done; "resolved," to use her therapist's favorite term. The nightmares were gone, the intrusive memories, startle response, all the things from the PTSD check-list ("Yes, waiter, I'll have one from column A, the nightmares sound good, and two from column B, a little avoidance of reminders would be nice, and, oh, why not?, one from column C, some self-blame will make for a nice desert.") were gone.

Still, from time to time she tested. Seeing the clearing, well, something reminds you, you check it out. Her grandfather was like that. He would not have understood the therapy but he would have understood stepping forward towards anything that might represent danger.

He was that kind. Odd that she thought of him. Maybe not so odd. Some of what he taught her stayed, giving her some strength in those times she needed it.

There were times when she likened herself to a sponge, recognizing that much of her strengths were absorbed from others, like her two friends who got her to go to therapy. When she wrote her story about them, the first one after they came back from the war, she learned from them. When everything happened, including the rape, she remembered them, drew on the lessons they taught, and copied the skills that enabled them to survive.

And she had.

She went back to work and poured herself into the work. She wasn't trying to escape anything, she was proving to herself she could do the work. But now it was all right. Nothing left to prove. Time to take a break, like anyone else. A clearing is a clearing is a clearing.

Ellen smiled. It was a sunny day. Time to walk back, maybe do some reading that had nothing to do with a news story.

And maybe find someone who liked running with his shirt off. She smiled again.

Bob Blasingame was not thinking about running with or without a shirt. He was rubbing his chin and studying a menu. The diner the police sergeant recommended was clean and bright. He was a little early for lunch but his morning tour of a pair of antique shops had gone well.

The waitress, a young woman who looked like she had graduated from high school earlier that summer, was patient with him. He looked up.

"I had a big breakfast," he said.

"Maybe just some pie?"

"That would be great. What would you recommend?"

"The apple is very good."

"I'll try it."

She smiled and took his menu.

There weren't many other people in the diner, probably a function of his early arrival. Now he sat at the counter, on the stool next to the cash register so the waitress kept returning.

The pie turned out to be more than very good.

"How is it?" she asked.

"Excellent," he said. He waited until she came back.

"I'm on vacation," he said. "Touring old buildings and antique stores."

"You are in the right place. This place has a ton of those."

"Heard about the plane crash. Sounded pretty bad."

"It was. Worst thing I ever saw."

"You were one of the volunteers that tried to help out?"

"Well," she paused. "I was there but I didn't do anything. I was just there."

"You didn't just go out there? That could have been dangerous with the fire and everything."

"No, no, I went with someone." She paused and smiled and waved at an older couple that came into the diner.

"One of the Johnston brothers? Someone told me they got there first and actually put out a fire."

"Put out a fire? Yes, I guess he did."

"Kind of a hero."

She said nothing. He took a sip of coffee and waited a moment before speaking again.

"I guess you were the first there."

"Yeah."

"By the way," he said, "I'm Bob Blasingame."

"Brenda," she said.

"Well, you take care," he said. He put five dollars down beside his cup and walked out.

Brenda watched him go and then pulled her phone from her pocket almost reflexively.

Blasingame walked down the street, past the municipal building, and then walked up the steps to a small, stone building that looked like it might have been designed by the same architect who built the first building he had seen. But rather than abandoned to vagaries of storage, this building had bright lights within and children's drawings in the windows.

He stepped in and paused as he looked around. The Coalville library was small but, in addition to shelves of books with narrow aisles, it had four computer stations. An older man sat at one, apparently viewing a website specializing in sports.

"Can I help you?"

A surprisingly young man walked up to Blasingame from the side.

"I hope so," Blasingame said. "I need to look up some news articles."

"Not a problem at all," the librarian said. "Let me get you started."

Ten minutes later, Blasingame was visiting the websites of numerous news organizations, with particular emphasis put on the local sources. He studied them intently, almost as if memorizing what he saw.

Almost everything he looked for had to do with the plane crash. The only thing that wasn't about the crash was something he looked for at the end, just before he thought he would leave.

He brought up a search engine and inserted "Ellen Parker" and "Philadelphia Enquirer." To his surprise, he had multiple hits; some, as he investigated, went back several years.

He read everything he could find and his eyebrows remained raised in mild surprise. Some of the articles were written by her; notes said two were nominated for Pulitzer prizes. Some of the articles were about her. They were stories he thought someone might turn into a Hollywood thriller. Shaking his head, he used Ellen's full name and searched Facebook and other social media.

She hadn't updated her Facebook entry for a couple of months. The last few status updates were thanks to people, including some relatives, and several statements that she was fine now, really.

Blasingame logged off and leaned back in the chair. A reporter? He had things to do and did not need someone looking over his shoulder. He nodded. It was good to be forewarned.

He stood up, waved to the librarian, and left the building.

He would keep an eye on Ellen Parker.

Radisson and Bornstein walked across the deserted yard. The house was in poor shape and weeds dominated the yard. Someone had tried flowers as a border but they were being defeated by the weeds.

Bornstein thought it showed Radisson's ability to plan; they didn't have anyone to question, but here they were, enjoying the Pennsylvania countryside as they used the online real estate listings to find a secluded place where such questioning could take place. The ducks were being put in a row. He grinned.

Radisson motioned with his head towards the Suburban, parked next to a weathered red and white *For Sale* sign.

"Hard to see the house from the road," he said.

Bornstein nodded and pointed ahead.

"I think the barn may be better."

It was. It was relatively small – it looked like it could hold a large piece of farm machinery but not much more - and made of steel sheeting on a concrete slab. The roll-up main doors were chained and padlocked but there was an unlocked door in the side. They went in and found it empty except for a row of wooden shelves up against the far wall. Bornstein had a small Maglite and swept the area.

"Looks good."

"Yes. Nice to have a chair."

"Maybe the house?"

They walked back to the house. It was locked and, peering through the front windows, they saw no furniture. However, on the back porch they found a pair of chairs, one a rocker, the other a heavy upright with arm rests.

"Perfect," Radisson said. He picked up the chair without assistance and held it in front of him as they walked back to the barn; Bornstein knew better than to ask if he needed help. He was stronger than he appeared.

"Exactly the furniture we needed," Bornstein said. "God is on our side."

"Hardly."

"If we get down to the Q and A, it's better than using someone's house, though we may have to go to it eventually."

"Only if we're told the case is there," Radisson said. "I hate questioning someone in their house." He shook his head. "Too much chance of people coming by. Interruptions. This is what we need."

"I agree." Bornstein paused. "You still think it's around here? It's been a month."

"It's here. You don't move something like the case unless you've gotten your buyer all set and if anyone had tried that anywhere on the East Coast or as far west as Chicago, Fredericks would know. There hasn't been a ripple."

"I hope you're right. Those people in Richmond…"

"Would sell their own mothers but no one's going to touch that case. Only a handful of people know what to do with it." He smiled. "And that includes us."

"You don't think anyone's going to suspect us? I mean, if our guy is as sharp as you say…"

Radisson paused at the driver's door.

"He might suspect, sure," he said. "But he won't be certain."

"So maybe he'll send someone to ask *us* questions."

"I already thought of that. We're going to leave him a trail. It'll point to whoever he has us talking to but it will look like we got there too late."

"Listen, Danny, I trust your judgment, you know that, but…" He paused. "Can you tell me the details?"

"Mikey, it's cool. Once we have our hands on the case, we move it immediately. FedEx it to San Diego."

Bornstein put his hands on the roof of the SUV.

"The Arab?" Bornstein's eyebrows went up.

"Exactly."

"I don't trust that bastard."

"Now you're being a racist. He knows what we're looking for. He already has a buyer. The money will be wired to our account, no one sees it. We go to Florida and gently tap into the cash as we wish."

"What if he doesn't send us the money?"

Radisson just smiled.

"All right," Bornstein said, "he knows better. But what if he decides to whisper in Frederick's ear, tries to score some points with our boss?"

"Makes himself complicit, if he does. If we go down, he goes down just as hard." His smile widened. "What, you think he talks to people, to the FBI, to

29

anyone? You can't do what he does if you can't keep your mouth shut. I chose him because he is squeaky clean. Anvil reliable."

"How big a cut is he getting?"

"A quarter."

Bornstein nodded. It was fair.

"All right, you're the boss. But that trail business, we have to have a good one if we're going to get people to go somewhere other than after us."

"We will. You put your finger on it. Richmond."

"No shit." Bornstein shook his head. "A lot of people don't like Richmond." He smiled. "If we tell our guy that the case went to Richmond…"

"Exactly. The Norfolk people, hell, the *Atlanta* people, everyone, will jump on Richmond and tear those pricks down. Fredericks will probably offer us a contract to go south again; a little icing for our retirement. Everyone's looking for an excuse. The whole East Coast will greenlight vaporizing them and Norfolk most of all. Norfolk thought their little gift was going to put them in good with Fredericks after all the bad blood. They'll be sweating teardrops and they'll be out to prove they're innocent. They'll lead the move on Richmond."

"Oh, yeah, they will. Considering how close Norfolk came to being burned flat… I get it. Sure, no one will find the case, or, at least, they'll say they didn't find the case, but we won't be in anyone's sights." Bornstein shook his head and grinned. "That's slick. What's the trail?"

"We keep it simple. We just say whoever we talked to said they took it to Richmond, to the handler who works for the Richmond people. He's not as connected as the Arab, but on the East Coast there are damned few who does what he does."

"All right, the Richmond angle works. But I see one possible flaw." Bornstein paused, thinking, and Radisson stifled his frustration. Sure, Bornstein kept hesitating but he had a good head (and gave good head, he thought and smiled). If he saw a flaw, it was worth listening to him.

"What is it?"

"To know about Richmond," Bornstein said slowly, "more specifically, to know about the guy who works for Richmond, he's got to be in the business. If whoever we talk to is just another civilian, no one will buy that he knows where to take the case. It's not like he could look up the guy's web page. A civilian wouldn't know who's handling hot trade in Virginia. Does that make sense?"

"Absolutely," Radisson said, nodding. He thought for a moment, then reached inside his jacket and pulled out his phone. "If it's a civilian or not, we get him to say whatever we want. We record it, so it's not just our word. Now, if he's a civilian, and, you're right, he probably will be, we'll get him to say something like a couple of weeks ago someone came looking for it, found him, and took it away. He will describe the guy. Guess who he will say he talked to?"

"No shit. The Richmond guy."

"Precisely. You know how Fredericks feels about all of those people in Richmond."

"Paranoid."

"What do you think he'll do when he hears the civilian talking?"

"He'll nuke the place from orbit. And you're right, we can do the same thing if he isn't a civilian, if he's in the business."

"If he's in the business, we get him to say he went down to Richmond himself. Either way. We record the whole thing. And that, ladies and gentlemen, is our trail."

"All right, let me think on this some more. See if I can punch any more holes in it."

"Be my guest." Radisson paused. "Mikey, you understand why I couldn't talk about all this with you before we left Albany?"

"You mean besides that we could barely get a moment alone with one another up there?" Bornstein shrugged. "I guess you did not have all the ducks lined up until we were on our way, so you didn't want to get me all eager and everything and then disappointed when a part fell through."

"You got it. I needed final confirmation from the Arab. I got it. We all right?"

"Yeah, we are. I trust you, man."

"Thanks."

"Fredericks wants us to drop the case off with the Harrisburg runner."

"Right. She probably feels like a yo-yo, waiting on the flight then going home and now she's told to get back on down to Harrisburg."

"Now she's back, waiting on us." Bornstein paused. "We're supposed to drop it off with her and then we go off on our retirement." He rubbed his chin, obviously still thinking.

"Yep. Fredericks' doing us a favor by not making us carry it all the way up to Albany."

31

"If your plan works, if he buys that Richmond stole it, he's going to ask us to hold off retiring. He'll want us to go after Richmond." He frowned.

"He might ask us and, if he does, we'll lend a hand. Keep him happy. But it's going to take him a while to get together with Norfolk and Atlanta, get clearance and all that. The case will already be on its way via those charming folks at FedEx."

"How long you think?"

"A week, I'd guess. That's how long it took to go after Norfolk in the first place."

"Yeah, I remember. All right, if our plan works, we may have a delay in taking off to Florida, you see?"

"Maybe, but maybe not. Fredericks may decide to go ahead without us. He won't be looking for people to do a lot of questioning and he's got several people who can burn the town down."

"Including our guy."

"Including our guy. If he asks, we go, but we stay cool, low profile. We keep ourselves alive."

"Sure, we're on the verge of retiring. No one's going to expect us to hit the place like a couple of mad dogs."

"Another payday, though."

"There's that."

After they got back into the car, Bornstein grinned.

"I know it's been done to death," he said, "but this is ironic."

"How's that?" Radisson carefully turned the large SUV around. "You're almost a hipster. 'Irony' is kind of in your territory."

"Shit, most of those kids confuse irony with stupidity. What I meant was we're just north of the crash site. It might even be on this place's property."

"Really?"

"Yep," he said, looking at his smart phone. "And lucky. This was the third place on the real estate listings. We might have had to go through a dozen before we found one that worked."

"Well, nothing is etched in stone. We can still use the woods if we have to."

"Just need a few minutes, I know. Still, it has its advantages, being indoors."

"North of the crash?" He looked both ways before turning onto the road. "How far?"

"If the listing is right, the site is either immediately adjacent to this property or actually on it. Less than a half mile."

"That's ironic, all right." Radisson smiled as he slipped his tinted shades on. "Maybe God is choosing sides after all."

Bornstein laughed and put his own sunglasses on. He liked Radisson's sense of humor.

There were rocking chairs on the porch of the main cabin. Ellen curled up in one after eating a granola bar, her Kindle balanced on her leg. She occasionally sipped on a glass of unsweetened tea. Patti and a young Hispanic woman moved from cabin to cabin. They were laughing about something when they finished. After they left, Ellen looked up and smiled. This seemed like the perfect place.

It was almost two o'clock when she heard her stomach growl and realized she was hungry. Another granola bar, starvation, or an early dinner? She weighed her options and finally settled on a quick run into town and a sandwich. Then she could snack out on wine and cheese in the evening. Tomorrow, she vowed, she would be sparing in her breakfast.

Really.

She did not get to her sandwich right away. As she drove into the town square, she saw a bookstore. Ellen maintained that books were, for her, an addiction – one of her friends at work suggested her collection of eBooks were a way of mainlining.

Well, maybe. But words… Since her childhood, reading opened doors to so much that she could not imagine being without them in whatever format. And bookstores were a rare treat.

She spent two hours and emerged with a shopping back holding several books. Ellen put the bag into her car and then she looked for a place to get something to eat.

Ellen saw the diner down the street and walked down to it. She took a seat in a booth and a young, blond waitress with the nametag of "Brenda." The young woman seemed a little distracted but took her order without an error.

She ate her turkey club while reading Robert Graves on her Kindle. The sandwich was pretty good but she lost track of it while following Claudius dodging Livia.

"Refill?"

Ellen looked up and saw the waitress. The woman must move like a cat.

33

"Sure," Ellen said and moved her glass closer. Brenda poured tea from a pitcher.

"Are you visiting people?"

"No," Ellen said. "I'm on vacation."

"You came to Coalville for a vacation?"

"I live outside Philly and wanted to spend more time relaxing than travelling."

Brenda thought for a moment.

"That's a pretty good idea," she said. "What are you doing?"

"Catching up on my reading and going for long walks. And leaving my phone off."

That got a smile from Brenda.

"I ought to copy you," she said.

"It really helps."

"Where are you staying?"

"Out at the Willow Run B and B."

"How is it out there?"

"I really like it. Next to the woods and they're nice to go into after so much time in the city. Quiet."

"What do you do in Philly?"

"I work for the Enquirer. The online side. Philly dot com."

"Really? That's awesome."

"It can be. Some days, though, it's a real drag."

"Was that something you had to go to school for?"

"I did, but I've met a lot of people working as journalists who majored in other things."

"I'm thinking of going to Delaware County Community College."

"I know it. What would you study?"

"I didn't do too well in high school so I need to kind of bear down and get a good foundation. Especially in science. Then maybe go and get a nursing degree."

"Nursing?"

"Yes. My Mom was a nurse. She passed two years ago. But she really liked it and everyone told me she was really good at it. I thought what she did was really awesome."

"What kind of nursing?"

"She worked pediatrics mostly."

"Well, I'm sorry to hear that she's passed, but I think she'd be happy to hear you want to do what she did."

"I think you're right. Did you become a reporter because someone in your family was one?"

"No," Ellen said, shaking her head. "My mother is at home. She was the one that raised us. My father was a real estate developer. I've got one uncle who's an engineer, another who's a university professor, a historian, and an aunt who is a professor, too, a psychologist. Her partner is a nurse. Works in an ER."

"Really? That's awesome. Did you always want to be a reporter?"

"I kind of backed into it. Originally I wanted to be a historian…"

"But reporting the news is history live, kind of. That's pretty neat."

"I like it," Ellen said.

The two women continued to talk, the subjects gently drifting from one thing to another. While doing so, they made a link, one that might, with time, turn into a friendship.

After some time, another woman came in and waved at Brenda.

"Hey, girl," the woman said. "Let me get my apron and I'll take it."

"Thanks, Janie," Brenda said. She turned back to Ellen. "Let me settle your bill."

Ellen paid her bill and said goodbye to Brenda. She left Brenda talking to Janie and was surprised to see the sky beginning to purple. She had spent far more time in the bookstore and the diner than she thought.

She drove back to Willow and spent several minutes examining the books she bought. They were all used – it gave her a sense of rescuing something when she bought a used book – and several were on historical subjects.

But her treasure, the one she started reading almost reflexively, was a library edition of Jules Verne's *20,000 Leagues Under the Sea*. Some pages were smudged but reading it was like plunging back into her childhood. Her aunt Catherine had given her a copy years before – it was long since lost – and it was still able to stir her imagination. Ellen read with a grin.

After a while she glanced outside and saw night had arrived. She remembered Patti's remark about wine and cheese and decided to give it a try. A small voice whispered to her that maybe Bob would be there and she smiled at herself.

The path to the main house was dark but the orange, glowing light of the big porch was inviting. Around her, scattered fireflies were rising, blinking information to one another that only they could understand. They made the forest's darkness part of the display and that made the shadows appear as things that might be worth investigating rather than avoiding.

Ellen had never been afraid of the dark. As a farm girl – more accurately, as a young girl who had spent as much time on her grandfather Tom's farm as she could – she had worked in the night, tending and moving animals, helping with the chores that had to be done before the next day arrived, and even the events of the last year had not taken that away from her.

She paused on the path to the main house to take a minute to admire the fireflies and listen to the night sounds. Somewhere two owls had a conversation and, after a moment, she thought she heard a fox bark. Taking that as a cue to continue, Ellen turned.

As she stepped on the gravel path, she saw an SUV come into the parking area in front of the house. It turned as it maneuvered, its headlights sweeping through the darkness. The vehicle stopped and, after a moment, Bob Blasingame slowly stepped out. Over his shoulder hung a camera bag. She walked forward and saw him take a cardboard box out of his vehicle.

Stopping at the porch, she saw him push close the car door with his hip and then turn toward the porch. He saw her and smiled, something she liked.

"Good evening," Blasingame said as he walked toward her.

"It is," Ellen said. "Are you coming back from an expedition?"

"I am a mighty hunter," he said, grinning. "I had some good luck with a few of the antique shops I visited. I haven't gotten to them all." He put the box down on the porch and then carefully placed the camera bag on top of it. "Are you going in?"

"I thought I'd give it a try."

"Sounds like a good idea." He looked down at the box and bag. "I doubt these will walk away. I'll take them to my cabin later."

"What are they?"

"Mostly brass hardware for windows but I found some old, hand-made iron hinges, probably for a barn door. Really neat stuff."

"They would be pretty rare, since most barn doors are sliders nowadays and have been for years, I think."

"You're right, at least for the heavy-duty kind. I think this," he paused and squatted down and pulled a black, massive hinge out with one hand while the other held the camera bag to one side, "is late Nineteenth Century." The hinge was obviously heavy but Blasingame handled it easily. He put it back down and stood up, slapping his hands together. "Careful, ma'am; I've been known to go into lecture mode with the slightest provocation."

"I'd like to hear it sometime," Ellen said. She gestured toward the door. "Shall we?"

"Sure." He followed her. "You know about farms?"

"Spent a lot of time on my Grandpa Tom's farm." She opened the door and the two entered the cabin.

One of the couples from the morning was already there, lounging on a plush couch with glasses of white wine on the table in front of them. Patti was not there but her partner Joyce was. At the moment, she sat across from the two men and she waved at Ellen and Blasingame.

"Welcome," she said. She waved towards the dining area. "Wines and juice, crackers and cheeses, there's a goat one from the farm west of here that the kids really like." As she spoke, a boy and girl emerged from the dining area with paper plates stacked with Ritz crackers and slices of cheese.

"Goats are cool," the boy said and the girl nodded.

"There you go," Joyce said. "That's got to be worth at least four stars in some review."

The children were followed by their father and he steered them toward a collection of well-padded chairs and footstools that looked like a small island in the room. The children and their father seemed to be having a private conversation as Ellen and Blasingame went into the dining area.

The wine, Ellen tried a glass of the white, was good, though she did not regard herself as an expert and knew that more than one glass made her very sleepy. The cheeses were of several kinds, each having a small card identifying it by type and source, and she tried to take one of each.

She and Blasingame took chairs around the low table in front of Joyce. She was in a conversation with the two men about a problem in gardening and they seemed to be agreeing on a couple of possible solutions. When there was a pause, Joyce introduced everyone. The two young men were Thomas and Steve. Then she turned to Ellen.

"How was your exploration of our woods?"

"Fine, great. It was a good day for walking."

"Did you get to the game lands? They are about a mile and a half in, kind of to the northeast."

"I saw the split in the path but I went the other direction, up the low hill."

37

"That's a nice way to go. On the other side of the hill, there are a couple of clear areas where they've put up bird houses, if you are a birder."

"I'll check them out."

"Watch out for rain. The weather is supposed to be scattered stuff over the next few days. And did you find any pirate treasure?" The question was directed at Blasingame.

"Just the odd doubloon," he said. "Not a peg leg to be seen."

Joyce laughed, something she did readily.

"He did find some things," Ellen said.

"Watch out," Joyce said. "Our antique shops can be addicting. We have more of them than churches."

"You do have some good ones," Blasingame said. "Antique shops, I mean. I don't know about the churches. Not just old chests of drawers. I'm mostly looking for things that could be used to restore older buildings and I've found two shops so far that have some of those things."

"Great. Patti said you are also taking pictures."

"A hobby at which I am pitiful." He gestured towards some of the photographs on the walls. "Nowhere near that level of quality."

"She said you were taking classes."

"Yep. I need all the help I can get."

"What kind of camera are you using?" Thomas asked.

"Canon digital," Blasingame said. "It's an EOS."

"Good camera," Thomas said. "I'm using a Nikon but it's just for work."

"He's a real estate agent," Steve said. "He takes pictures of property for sale and they put them online."

"I'd like to use it for other stuff, like birding. But I'm not terribly good at it."

"I'm the same way," Blasingame said. "Most of my shots are of old buildings but I really want to learn how to use it for other things. I'm taking classes. Adult ed thing at my local community college."

"That sounds like a good idea. Where are you from?"

"New York, near Albany."

"Came a long way."

"I'm hoping to get over to Lancaster in the next few days. Hit the antique stores and take pictures of the Amish farms and covered bridges."

"We're antiquers," Steve said. "Can't turn down a good bargain."

"He just wants," Thomas said, smiling, "to get on the *Antique Road Show*."

Steve laughed and Joyce joined in. She turned to Blasingame.

"You were at the crash site, I hear."

"You did? Ah, lawyer." Blasingame nodded. "You have contacts among the police. Yes, I was. Met a Sergeant Peterson there. I was getting shots of the plant growth trying to come back from the fire. I want to use that kind of rebirth as a project for class."

"Mike's a good guy," Joyce said. "He told me when I ran into him at the courthouse. You told him you were staying here, so it came up while we were talking. That seems like an interesting project."

"Well, I think I'm still trying to get my head around it. A real tragedy and I felt a little bit like I was intruding. But it did seem to bring out the best in people. I heard about all the local folks who responded and tried to help. It reminded me of what happened after 9/11."

"It seemed like half the town was there," Joyce said, nodding.

"Were you there?"

"I was. I got there about the same time as the fire company and there were already people there."

"What was everyone doing? I was told a couple of brothers got there first and one of them actually put out a fire."

"That would be Fred Johnston. He and his brother Carl got there first, I think. Most people were looking around for survivors. After the fire was pretty well put down, those who stayed were organized into search groups to mark where bodies were."

"Sounds rough."

"I think most everyone just wanted to do something to help and setting markers for them seemed to be the least we could do." She paused. "We ran out of markers." She fell silent and no one spoke for a moment.

"I'm sure all of that was appreciated by the families," Blasingame said.

"I hope so."

"I'm sure of it." Again no one spoke.

"What happens to the families?" Thomas asked. "I mean, when something like this happens, what do they do?"

"Mostly," Blasingame said, "they wait. In something like a plane crash, the National Transportation Safety Board takes over and everything, even the dead, are regarded as possible evidence, so there's a formal protocol that's followed that integrates the local services like hospitals. For families, that means there may be a delay as the bodies are examined. Everyone moves things as fast as they can, but they don't want to overlook anything."

"I think I can see that. Same with luggage and personal possessions, I guess."

"Same principles but the luggage always takes longer, sometimes months."

"Why?"

"Every piece has to be examined, weighed, tested. They can let families know what they've found if there are intact nametags, of course, but it can be a while before they release something." He shrugged. "They can't be sure that they are done with the luggage until they are pretty well done with the whole investigation. Maybe there's a point where they begin to suspect that some system failed and have to go back to the luggage and other material from the crash to see if there's any evidence of that failure. You know, like stains from a hydraulic leak."

"Sounds like you know about that stuff."

"Oh, there's a lot on the internet about it." He paused again before turning to Joyce. "You mentioned Fred Johnston. Do you know who else got there before the crowd?"

"Actually," Joyce said, "as best I remember from what people said, the Johnstons were first. Then everyone else arrived almost together. People were doubling and tripling up in pickups and cars to get there, so we all came in kind of like a flood, all at once. Dwayne Richards, he's the Assistant Fire Chief, he got everyone organized, made us all into teams of a half dozen so no one would be by themselves. Later on, those teams were joined together when the recovery effort was made. He kept an eye on us all."

"Good move," Blasingame said.

"Do they know what caused the crash?" Ellen asked. "The last I read, they suspected that it was a fire in an engine."

"I think they still believe that," Joyce said. "Someone said it might have been the hydraulics around the engine having something to do with it but they are still looking."

"Some jobs suck worse than mine," Steve said.

"What do you do?" Blasingame asked.

"I'm a social worker," he said. With that the conversation turned away from the crash and journeyed through social work to community services, large and small, and went back to photography. Blasingame and Thomas walked around the cabin, looking at the prints and Steve followed them. Joyce started cleaning up but left the opened bottles out after wrapping the cheese.

"See you tomorrow," Joyce said to Ellen as she got to the door. "Hope you dodge the rain tomorrow."

"It'll be all right," Ellen said. "I know we need it."

Eventually, Steve and Thomas went off to their cabin and Blasingame sat next to Ellen. She noticed that he had barely touched his wine all evening.

"Not very good?" she asked.

"Oh, it's fine," he said. "I don't think I've fully accepted being on vacation so I'm not letting myself relax." He smiled as he looked at his glass. "I'll take this with me when I go back to my cabin. I still have to take some pictures of the things I found to send to a client back home."

"I can help you carry things. More than you can do with just two hands if you are going to also take your wine glass."

"Great," he said. They both stood and he led the way to the porch.

He handed Ellen his glass, slung the camera bag strap over his shoulder and carefully picked up the box.

"Let's do it," he said and led the way to the cabin path.

He looked over his shoulder as they walked.

"You seem to be totally into being on vacation," he said. "How do you do it?"

Ellen made a short laugh.

"Maybe I just really needed it."

"You're not trying to find a story to write up?"

"Oh, no, not me. I've kept my Wi-Fi and phone off. Just me and the Willow Run B and B."

"That's the way to do it," Blasingame said. "Sometimes you just have to push everything else away and take care of yourself. I've got to practice that. Here we are."

He put the box down, opened his cabin, and turned to Ellen.

"Thanks for the assistance," he said as he reached for the wineglass.

"Glad to help out," she said. "Have a good night." She turned and went to her cabin.

Ellen sat on the bed in her cabin and looked at her hand. It had brushed Blasingame's when he took his glass and there had been... What? A tingle? Something. She smiled as she shook her head.

What are you thinking, girl?

Day Three

Chapter 3

The morning was colder than the day before and revealed the culprit to be the jumbled, lumpy, dark gray mass of clouds hiding the sun. Pennsylvania was doing its usual guessing game about rain and Ellen, though tempted, did not allow the threat to keep her from her morning run.

She ran to the road and back but did not see Blasingame. He did not appear during her second lap so Ellen decided to follow the path into the forest she had walked the day before. The exploration, at least as far as the clearing, had revealed the path to be without ankle-endangering traps and she liked being off the road.

An estimate, based on what her legs told her, had her about a kilometer into the woods when she saw three deer. They did not seem startled to see her, though they were only a few yards from her path. They watched her, their dark eyes revealing nothing but seeming to see, Ellen thought, everything about her.

She kept her running rhythm, thinking that they would run away if she stopped. They continued to watch, their heads turning, their eyes on her. There was no judgment but it felt like they were totally aware of her and who she was.

Ellen knew on one level she projected her own thoughts and feelings onto the animals but, nonetheless, their calm gaze seemed to be reassuring.

We know where you've been and where you are. You're all right. Now, just move along, we want to eat.

The last sentence in her head brought a smile to her face, balancing a quick, small arrival of tears that just as quickly blinked away. As she left the deer behind, a glance over her shoulder revealed they were back at their breakfast.

And what interpretation do you make of that, that a bunch of grass is of more significance than you?

Ellen grinned. Maybe it was so. Maybe.

And where was Bob? And why did she care? Ellen's grin broadened, remembering the picture of the man's back as he ran. It was a... *Nice* image.

And what was also nice was realizing such pictures were something she could see again.

Ellen, still smiling, picked up her pace.

Bob Blasingame was in Coalville, parked outside the diner. He had skipped his morning exercises to get to the diner early. The morning crowd was well entrenched, getting breakfast before going to work or wherever they had to go at the start of the day.

He could see Brenda and another girl moving among them. Brenda seemed routinely to smile as she talked to the customers, though the smile faded when she talked to two men at a table adjacent to a window.

One man, the older, maybe in his late thirties, was beefy and had closely cropped hair over a reddish face, and sat with his hands folded in front of his face, his sleeves rolled up revealing faded tattoos.

The man across from him was younger, about Brenda's age, and wore his dark brown hair longer in a wave across his forehead He had dark eyes with arching eyebrows and his narrow nose sat over a straggly moustache that did not enhance his face. Like the older man, he parked his hands in front of his mouth.

Brenda poured their coffee, her expression blank with close-cropped, relaxing a little with long-hair, but leaving before saying anything.

Blasingame looked at both men carefully, comparing them to images he had on his smart phone, images he had gathered from the web page of the "Johnston Brothers Garage." He was looking at, he decided, Fred and Carl Johnston.

The pictures of the two men matched pictures he saw when researching the volunteers at the crash site. He had found them, though they had not been identified, in the background of a picture showing a firefighter directing a group of the volunteers to one side, towards something in the darkness.

In the picture, one of a series not published in its print editions but left on the *Daily Local's* website, the younger brother, Carl, wore a backpack.

Blasingame thought that picture was very interesting.

"All right, I'll tell him," Michael Bornstein said, nodding and speaking into his phone. "And do we…? I understand. We got it. Do you want me to call you back or him? You? All right. Anything else? Yes, of course, we want to move fast. All right. Talk to you."

"What's up?" Radisson asked as his partner put his phone away. He was doing crunches on the floor of their motel room.

"That was Mr. Fredericks."

"Not our boy?"

"No. He talked with Fredericks and Fredericks decided to talk to us directly."

"Our guy needed a decision from Fredericks, I guess, since we're in Mr. Books' territory. What do they want us to do?" He had stopped his exercises and was lying flat on his back, his hands behind his head.

"He wants us to get to a man and get some questions answered. He thinks the man, a local, may have taken the case."

"Shit, that's impressive. Our guy is moving quick. Who do they want us to talk to?"

"Man named Fred Johnston. He owns a garage on the north side of town. Mr. Fredericks says our guy thinks he and his brother, he's named Carl, got to the plane and stole the case. They are going to try to get us more information about the two, so he's going to call Books about them, see if there's any reason to hesitate. If he's a professional thief, maybe he's one of Books' people."

"Good to know who we're going after."

"You still want to take a run at hanging onto it?"

"We've been over this. We're the ones talking to Johnson…"

"Johnston. With a T."

"Whatever the fuck. Johns*ton*. We're the ones getting the answers. We pick up the case and we say it looks like it went to Richmond. We get a recording. No one knows what we know." He paused, understanding Bornstein's anxiety. Yes, this could be very dangerous.

"See, what we know now helps us," Radisson said. "There's two of them. Corroboration. Regardless of who says what, we'll say the first one gave us the other."

"His brother?"

"Right, but doesn't know what his bro did with it. Then we talk to Johnston number two and that's the one who says it went to Richmond. We'll have talked with both of them, got them both recorded, saying what we want them to say. We'll know where it is and have everyone else chasing geese." He paused again, seeing Bornstein frowning slightly. "What you got, Mikey?"

"The recordings are key to the whole thing," Bornstein said. "We can't forget them."

"Absolutely right. We can't just say they said nothing; no one will believe we got nothing from them."

"We're pretty good at getting answers." Bornstein smiled softly.

"Right.

"Helps our retirement fund."

"Big time."

"All right," Bornstein said. "Let's give it a run."

"Think Hinckley *Picnic* boat."

"Think a pair of them. The case, you know?"

"Oh, yeah. A pair *easily*."

Ellen finished breakfast just as the rain began. Patti looked out the window, glancing up at the sky, and shook her head.

"I don't think it's going to last," she said.

"Famous last words," Steve said and Thomas grinned as he finished his coffee.

"You two still going into Philly?"

"Yep." Steve glanced at his wrist. "We can catch the train down at Thorndale if we get rolling."

"I'm waiting on you," Thomas said, standing up. "Some people are sluggards."

Steve stuck out his tongue, waved to Ellen and Patti, and, pulling on a windbreaker, followed Thomas out of the cabin.

"You going into the woods for another hike?" Patti asked.

"I was going to go into town. You mentioned the antique shops."

"Anything in particular you looking for?"

"I'd like to find a nice desk for writing. Any recommendations?"

"Two places are pretty big on furniture items. Let me write the addresses." She disappeared into the kitchen and raised her voice. "The first one is a little pricey but usually has a good selection. The other's smaller but more reasonable." She came back and handed Ellen a small piece of notepaper. "Tell Kelly, he has the larger store, I recommended him."

"I'll get a discount?"

"He may throw you out," Patti said in mock seriousness. "But he may avoid trying to sell you everything else in the shop."

Ellen smiled at the joke and, a few minutes later, was in her car and headed for town. She stopped in front of the smaller antique store first as the rain faded into a slight mist.

The store was not very wide but it extended further than she expected. While they had many chests of drawers, shelves, and end tables, the only desks they had were pretty ornamental with small tops.

"Well," the clerk, a tall, thin white man said, "I can keep an eye out and let you know if we find anything closer to what you want."

"That would be great. Here's my card." He took it and examined it for a moment.

"You came a way to see our store."

"I'm on vacation," she said. "Over at Willow."

"Joyce and Patti's." He nodded, still reading the simple card. "She, Joyce, did some work for me when I bought this store." He looked up. "Are you with Mr. Blasingame?"

"No. He's there, too."

"Yes. Looking for things for rehab. Nice guy, seems like. Interested in the crash. Asked me if I'd been out there. Hadn't."

"He's doing some photo class project."

"That's what he said," the man agreed, slipping the card into his shirt pocket. "You have a good day, now, and I'll keep you in mind."

"Thank you."

The mist was reluctant to leave and Ellen flipped on her wipers while making her way across the square and then down a street to the other antique store Patti recommended. She parked and reached for her bag. The drawstring had come loose and her phone spilled out as she lifted the bag.

Ellen closed the bag and stuffed the phone into her jeans pocket after making sure it was off. She had promised she would check for messages "every so often" and had managed not to do so since arriving at Willow. Maybe tonight. One-time check, no call-backs.

She grinned at herself and her effort to remain out of sight and mind and walked into the store.

It was bigger than the first one but not by much. Wider and better lit, it also extended deeply into the block. She stood at the door wondering what it had been in its first incarnation.

"Stable," a man said from her right. He was black and had curly hair that hung around his ears which were pierced by several small earrings. "In back,

47

that was a blacksmith shop. They merged almost two centuries ago and then the original wood walls were replaced by stone. I think they needed to support the common roof. Everyone asks."

"Thanks. I was wondering why it didn't hit the building behind."

"No building to hit, not ever. And the cross street isn't that far away. Are you looking for something specific or just on a voyage of discovery?"

"Well, I'm looking for a working desk and Patti said you might have them. Are you Mr. Kelly?"

"Kelly's my first name. But she spoke of me? Patti? Heart of my heart, soul of my soul, she is." He clutched his heart.

Ellen chuckled.

"No," he said, motioning her to follow, "this isn't any of your tawdry, cheap lust. This is pure love, an affair of angels. We meet on a spiritual plane that few mortals can imagine."

"I suspect Joyce would have a thing or two to say about that." He turned and raised his eyebrows.

"Kentucky?"

"Ohio."

"Southern Ohio, then."

"Yes."

"Good to hear your voice, ma'am. I'm from Youngstown."

They shook hands and he bowed slightly.

"I immigrated to Philadelphia twelve years ago."

"Why was that?"

"I came for the waters."

"But there are no waters in Philadelphia," Ellen said with mock seriousness, recognizing the line from *Casablanca*.

"I was misinformed," he said. "Came for school and stayed for the antiques. You?"

"Kind of the same. Got hired by the Enquirer a few years ago and work on…"

"Philly dot com," he said. "I think I know you. Know *of* you." He kept walking and turning through the furniture. "You won a Pulitzer on those military women."

"Nominated, just nominated."

"It was a very good article," Kelly said and the bantering tone that was a part of his normal conversation was gone. "People putting their lives on the line like that and then running into all that crap when they get home. One of these days we're going to wake up and find we don't have any soldiers when we need them. Here we go, take a look at this."

He swept his hand in front of him.

"Nineteenth Century, Pennsylvania, slant top desk. Collector's item."

"Can't use it," she said. "Need to be able to work on it. Computer, books."

"Ah," he said, nodding, "functional. I may have a deal for you. Let me show you."

Kelly led her further into the back until they were in shadows and almost at the rear. He turned up the lights and pulled a sheet off a large rectangle.

"Here we go. Desecrated, but you might like it. Fourth quarter of the Nineteenth Century. Big, flat surface, 54 inches wide, 36 deep. Walnut with burl inserts. The pedestals have four drawers on the right and, on the left, look, two deep drawers faced to look like the four on the right. Cool, right?"

"It looks great. You said 'desecrated'?"

"It was refinished maybe twenty years ago. The old patina was cleaned off..."

"Ouch."

"Yeah, really. Refinished. But that's not the worst." Kelly stepped closer and pointed.

"It was a roller desk," he said, frowning and shaking his head. "It had, if it was done by the same cabinet maker as one I sold last year and I think it was, a beautiful combination of small shelves and drawers and pigeon holes along with the segmented S-roll top. And some idiot sheered it all off to gain a couple more square inches of desktop. Maybe back in the Fifties. Here, look at it from this angle. See the edges, how different that looks across the back and on the sides? Sure, the idiot sanded it down and then re-stained the whole top but you can still see where the surgery was done. And the staining doesn't match the rest of the desk." He seemed close to being angry.

"I see what you mean," she said, bending as she studied it.

"I had a pro look at it," Kelly said. "Fellow down near Kennett Square who's my go-to guy for restoration. He almost wept." He shook his head. "You don't want it for display, you want to work with it."

"Right."

"You might be better off with Ikea."

"Or milk crates with boards."

"That would work."

"Not what I want."

"Why not?"

"I want something made by someone," Ellen said. "Not from an assembly line. That has its place but I have that at work. At home, well…" Her voice trailed off.

"A reporter without words," Kelly said, the bantering back but gentled by his smile. "You want to work on something that has felt the pen and paper of someone who wrote, something that was built by someone who cared about what he was doing. Because you do."

"Pretty close," she said. Ellen cocked her head to one side. "Do you write?"

"Only about this," he said, waving his hand around. "Articles for antique magazines and sites, that kind of thing. Now, do you want to know how much this is?"

"I'll hold my breath. Ready."

"With the roller and original finish and patina, an easy five thousand."

"I'm still here."

"But in its present shape, without the roller, with the terrible staining that was done to it, the scarring, I'm going to have to make a major investment to restore it, and even then, with the loss of the original roller top, it would come in a lot lower than that. So, I'll let you have it for two."

"Let me breathe for a moment. Do you deliver?"

"Of course. Are you going to haggle?"

"No. I'll give it a good home."

"I believe you. All right, eighteen hundred, not a dime more."

"Excuse me?"

"Seventeen if I can come and take pictures of it when you get it home. I want to use them in an article."

"An article?"

"In this business," he said, "lots of people buy things for investment, for decoration, for the mini-museums they've turned their houses into. But this," he lightly tapped the desktop, "was made by someone who expected it to be used. Beautiful, yes, but beauty that was supposed to be used. Beautiful because that would make the work easier, you see? I'm writing an article on that subject. So, if you are going to use it, work on it, sweat over it, then you are doing what that man more than a century ago wanted to have happen. Let me take pictures."

"Deal," Ellen said, and held out her hand. Kelly smiled and shook it.

"Deal," he said. "Now, take a moment and explore it. See if you can find the secret hidey-hole."

Ellen opened all the drawers and looked in the well but Kelly had to show her how to tap the back of a drawer. She smiled, delighted at the secret.

They processed her credit card and arranged for delivery. Ellen waited while a surge in the rain passed overhead. They talked as they watched the rain.

"Have you met Mr. Blasingame?" Kelly asked. "He's out at Willow Run."

"Yes. He's vacationing, too."

"Restoration guy. We get a few here, but I don't have a lot of building materials."

"He's picked up a lot of door brass and iron so far."

"Good. I thought he was some kind of news person or just a ghoul. Maybe those are the same thing."

"Oh, I see – you've made your sale and now you're going to make fun of my profession."

Kelly laughed.

"Well, he's not a ghoul. He asked about the crash. Then he explained about this camera project he's doing."

"For his class."

"Right. Rebirth of life kind of thing. Nice idea. He asked me if I had gone out there as one of the volunteers and I had to tell him that I wasn't. Not a civilian volunteer, I mean. Bless their hearts. It was a bad thing."

"You saw it?"

"I'm an EMT with our ambulance crew. That's what I meant. I was there but I wasn't a civilian. I was standing outside the firehouse bay, just finished some maintenance, talking to a couple of firefighters when we heard it. The aircraft, I mean; loud, but didn't see it. The fireball, yes. We were rolling quick." He paused. "It was pretty awful."

"It sounds like half the town came out to help."

"Some were there before us, down at the far end. They went right over the barbed wire fence, didn't hesitate." He paused again. "Rain's letting up. Let me get you an umbrella and you can get into your car."

"You don't have to do that."

"My pleasure." He went behind the counter and came back with an umbrella and then stopped in place, smiling as he looked out the front.

51

"If I knew that was all it took," he said. Ellen turned and looked. The rain had stopped while the gray clouds were giving way, if not to blue sky, then at least letting bright silver define their edges.

"Like magic," she said.

"Say hello to Patti for me," Kelly said, opening the door and glancing upward. The clouds were moving and becoming brighter.

"I will," Ellen said stepping outside. Kelly walked with her the few steps to her car, his eyes still on the sky. He held the umbrella as if not trusting the weather. It being Pennsylvania, Ellen thought, that was probably a good move.

"Willow Run's a pretty nice place," she said.

"If Gays ever need an Underground Railroad," he said, "it will be a stop. Oh, not because you can hide there but because Joyce makes such great breakfasts." He nodded. "The whole Gay movement is about finding good places to eat – forget everything you've heard about politics, marriage, and civil rights. I've been telling all my Republican friends that, if they ever have a really good meal, they'll be more than half way to being Gay." He nodded again, his voice serious. "I have them terrified of going anywhere except McDonald's."

"That's a terrible thing to do," Ellen said as she got into her car.

"Possibly. Have a safe drive back." He tapped the roof of her car as she backed out.

Minutes later, just outside of Coalville, Radisson and Bornstein saw Ellen's car drive past but made no comment; it was just another Honda. With their own car pulled over into the shoulder's trees, they had seen several cars pass in the rain. They were far enough off the road that the passing drivers did not take much notice of them.

To the people in the garage they watched, they and their car were almost invisible. In spite of the rain, one of the bay doors was left up. With the other one down, Bornstein thought the building looked like it was winking. Radisson said there wasn't much of anything to really make it look like a face but that had been the total of their conversation for the past two hours.

Bornstein's phone buzzed and he answered. Radisson listened, but his eyes stayed on the garage and the movement of someone around a tow truck. Bornstein shut his phone off and shook his head.

"It just gets better and better," he said.

"What's up?" Radisson raised a small pair of binoculars, a brand favored by birders, identified the person at the truck as being the younger Johnston, Carl, and put the binoculars down.

"That was Fredericks. Talked with Books. Books knows the Johnstons."

"Don't tell me they work for him." He shook his head.

"Peripheral actors. Mostly Fred. Carl less so. Fred did a nickel in Graterford, that's a prison, trafficking in stolen property, something like that."

"Do people really say that, someone 'did a nickel'?"

"I heard it on *The Wire*, I think."

"Good show. So, are we still clear or what?"

"We are still good to go. He just wanted to update us. Fred's been used for moving things."

"Drugs?"

"Didn't say."

"Drugs."

"And he's a bad actor."

"Really? A tough guy?"

"Books apparently thinks he has anger management issues."

"He didn't say that."

"Scout's honor, that's what Fredericks said he said."

"'Anger management issues.'" He shook his head. "I'm pretty sure they didn't talk like that on *The Wire*."

"He'll have a gun nearby, is also what he said."

"There goes the tow truck. I don't see anyone else."

"I think it is time for us to talk with Fred."

Radisson started the car, checked the traffic, and pulled out onto the road. It was barely two hundred yards to the garage and he did not hurry.

"Remember the thing about the gun issue," Bornstein said, releasing his seatbelt as they pulled into the garage's parking area.

"Got it."

Radisson stopped the car neatly between two white lines and paused as he got out of the car to look around. Bornstein stepped away from the car, his sport coat open but his hands at his sides as he took a position where he could see the side of the garage.

The garage looked to be in good shape; well-lit, it was clean. A green car sat in the open bay but there was no one with it. Radisson walked across the garage and saw Fred behind the counter. He checked the far side of the building but there was no one. He put on a smile as Fred looked up and walked into the office.

He was still smiling as he walked up to the counter. Bornstein followed him but kept his eyes outside.

"Clear," Bornstein said. Immediately Radisson had a pistol in Fred's face.

"On the floor," he said and when Fred, his hands lifting from a keyboard, hesitated, Radisson whipped the pistol across his face. "On the floor," he repeated.

He did not try to knock Fred unconscious; unlike the movies, in real life such blows had a good chance of badly damaging someone, even killing them, and he needed Fred alive and coherent.

For a while, anyway.

Radisson, his hand with the pistol hovering above Fred's neck, did a quick pat down of the man's sides and back and then secured his wrists together with police-grade handcuffs. He pulled Fred to his feet and then checked his front. There were no weapons but, as he turned to bring Fred around the counter, he saw a pistol under the counter. He shook his head. Amateur.

"Are we still clear?"

"Yes."

They took Fred through the garage for the concealment it offered in case someone drove by but no one did. Bornstein went first and opened the door of the Suburban and climbed in. Radisson guided Fred in and waited while his partner covered Fred's mouth with duct tape and pushed him down into the foot well.

"Big mistake if you move," Bornstein said, lightly tapping the back of Fred's head with his Glock. Radisson closed the door and got behind the wheel. In a moment, they headed north, toward the crash site and the barn beyond.

Blasingame stopped at a few more antique stores, though he found little that held his interest. One dealer tried to get him interested in some book shelves but he gently disengaged himself.

Every place he stopped, Blasingame asked about the crash and who had gone to it. He heard nothing that he had not learned before.

But Coalville was not a large town and the antique shop owners all knew one another. During the day they talked to one another, at the diner, while visiting each other's shops, at one of two bars. They all let each other know a man was down from New York looking for material for restoration projects of old buildings and mentally ran through their inventories as they heard.

Most of the people Blasingame talked to also mentioned, just to fill the conversation opportunity, that he seemed interested in the crash. Well, sure, it was the biggest thing to happen in northern Chester County. But, no, it was a little more than that. He was interested in who had gone to it.

Some wondered why for a short period of time and then they went back to their club sandwiches, or visiting, or beers while watching the Phillies drop one. One of them, sitting at the diner counter and sliding her empty iced tea glass back, mentioned it to Sergeant Michael Peterson, who put down his cup of coffee, cocked his head to one side, and wondered why.

He did so for more than a short period of time.

What they did to Fred Johnston was not bloody but very painful. Blood, and its accompanying DNA, could end up in the damnedest places, as both Radisson and Bornstein knew from their youth. Leaving his wrists handcuffed behind him, they duct-taped Johnston to the heavy chair and put a plastic dry-cleaning bag over his head and let his lungs burn with accumulated carbon dioxide.

The pain was the body's own warning system that it was not getting enough oxygen. It escalated rapidly while waves of panic slammed through Johnston until he passed out.

The first time they did it, they asked no questions. They wanted him to know what it was going to be like and that they controlled whether or not he would wake up from each trial.

And they did it because they liked to. Then they asked their questions.

"You stole something from the crash," Radisson said. He was very calm. "We want it back."

"I don't know what you are talking about."

The last half of his sentence was partially muffled by the bag that Bornstein slipped over his head. He gathered up the slack and twisted it, sealing the bag shut around the man's neck. They let him almost slip into unconsciousness before removing the bag and gave him a minute to gasp.

"God…" Johnston said. His eyes were closed and his head was bent forward. "God." His voice was raw.

"Not the answer," Radisson said. "We want the case you stole."

Fred Johnston was, as the communication from Books through Fredericks had suggested, a tough guy. But, as anyone who ever had to hold their breath for a very long time could attest, what he went through rapidly became overwhelming. His panic increased from his desperate attempts to breathe – inhaling and exhaling did nothing to reduce the fire in his lungs and they burned hotter and hotter.

It took four tries. Johnston was crying, which Bornstein found a little embarrassing. The man's nose was running and he drooled without noticing. It was, Bornstein thought, a sloppy display. But then, everyone they ever did this to ended up looking the same, though some went longer than four. Radisson's latex gloved hand pushed Johnston's head up, carefully using his forehead.

"Again," he said. Radisson was smiling, though he was unaware of it. "Where is the case?"

"I don't know," Johnston said, despair slurring his words. "Carl... I told Carl to hide it. Please..."

Radisson looked at Bornstein who, thinking, shrugged and then nodded. Radisson returned the nod and pulled off his latex gloves. Then he brought out his phone. He held it up for a second and Bornstein smiled.

"We'll keep it simple," Radisson said. He tapped the screen and then held it close to Johnston. "Where is the case?"

"I don't know. I told you. I gave it to Carl, told him to hide it."

Radisson tapped the screen again and then held the phone to his ear. He smiled softly.

"Got it," he said to Bornstein. "We're done here."

The phrase was a traditional one they used and was a signal to Bornstein. He put the bag over Johnston's head one last time, tied off the slack in a knot rather than just held it, and stepped back. Johnston, his eyes wide and his face one of horror as he realized what was coming, tried to jerk himself free of the chair.

Bornstein and Radisson stood to one side as Johnston's spasms became weaker.

"You want to hear it?" Radisson tapped the screen and handed the phone to Bornstein. He listened for a few seconds.

"Perfect," he said. He handed the phone back. "We'll get Carl to name Richmond. This is simpler."

"Quicker." Radisson said, putting the phone into his jacket. His eyes never left Johnston and he waited until there were no more movements, no attempt to breathe oxygen that wasn't there. He waited a few seconds more and then felt Johnston's wrist.

His fingers touched the other wrist and finally the side of the neck. Nodding, he removed the handcuffs – you can always find a use for a good set of 'cuffs.

"All right," he said, pocketing the handcuffs. "Let's go see if we can find brother Carl."

"Sounds like a plan."

Blasingame was in the main house as Ellen drove up. He walked to the door and held it open as she came across the porch.

"Good day?" he asked.

"Bought a desk," she said. "Got it from Kelly."

"I met him, I think," Blasingame said as he followed her in. "Tall, black man?"

"That's him." Ellen dropped onto the couch. "It was beat-up but is basically solid."

"He seemed to have a lot of furniture. Was it a real antique?" He sat down on the couch.

"Yes, but it had been mistreated. I think he figured the price of restoring it was going to be a bit much for what he could get back so I got a pretty good deal."

"Excellent."

"And how has your day been? Find anything?"

"Found some buggy tie-offs that used to be on the side of a Quaker meeting house. I don't know if any of my clients can use them, but I couldn't pass them up."

"Seduced by antiques. It's a terrible fate."

"I did get a lead on a possibility. There's a contractor south of town, near Parkesburg. Someone suggested him and I gave him a call. He's got things from tearing down some old buildings. Barns and houses. I'll swing by tomorrow."

"I'll keep my fingers crossed for you."

"Thanks." Blasingame smiled and Ellen noticed it was a nice smile. "Do you have plans for dinner?"

"Well, no, not really."

"Well, Alfredo's is supposed to be nice. I haven't tried it yet. Would you like to go with me?"

"Yes. That sounds fine."

"I don't know what the crowds are like there. Maybe we should go on the early side, say in an hour?"

Ellen glanced at her watch and nodded.

"That will work," she said, standing. He stood and there was a moment as their eyes met and the silence seemed to draw out. Then she smiled and left.

It was after she finished her shower that Ellen tapped the face of her cell phone. There were text messages, of course, and indicators of several messages, all of which she refused to look at as she hurriedly scrolled down – they all seemed to be from people at work and she felt virtuous by not giving into temptation. Then one popped into her vision.

From: Karen Deevers

Ellen paused. The messages from work, well, it was an unwritten rule that the only thing anyone sent to someone on vacation were jokes and videos of kittens, a rule that did not hold to head editors but none of them had sent her anything.

Karen, on the other hand, was a charter member of the "Shot to Hell Club" she, Ellen and two other women had formed the previous year. A good friend, Karen was an FBI agent whose path had crossed Ellen's first when she was a child. Most recently, they tried to help a woman protect a child – in the process, Karen was shot in a pizza restaurant parking lot while taking down a professional killer and Ellen… She started to bite down on the memory but realized it no longer was something she had to hide from.

Part of the memory included Ellen's final confrontation with a serial murderer in a clearing not far from the Willow Run Bed and Breakfast. Geography, she realized, probably was one reason for coming here. Karen knew she was on vacation. Her friends in the STHC were an exception to the rule, she decided, and tapped the message. It was short.

Call me.

She did. Deevers' FBI office phone flipped her to her cell and Ellen heard her pick up on the second ring.

Deevers.

"So how's your love life?" Ellen grinned as she asked; Karen's husband, once upon a time, had been an Ohio county deputy sheriff where Ellen lived years before. Now he was a lawyer and landlord and joked about holding down two of the three most despised professions in America.

I have him cornered, as you well know. And yours?

"Mm, looking the field over."

At a B and B noted for being 'gay friendly?' Are you thinking of switching?

"How did you know about Willow Run?"

FBI, remember? We know everything, or at least know how to pretend we do. Are the breakfasts as good as their website says?

"I'm putting on tons. What's up? I," she paused for dramatic effect, "have a date."

The recklessness of youth. I called to let you know I was coming out to Coalville tomorrow. Maybe we can grab lunch?

"Love to. I know a nice diner just off the square."

I see it on my map. One all right?

"Sure." She paused; she knew better than to ask what was going on, but…

This will be off the record, anything we might discuss. Just in case you were thinking.

Ellen sighed. Well, this was supposed to be a vacation, not work.

"And so another Pulitzer slips away," she said. "How is JJ?"

He's on the ACLU board and delighted – they're suing Philly PD for arresting some people who were taking videos of officers in public. Don't you read your own newspaper?

"Not for several days now. It's wonderful."

Not even a peek?

"Not yet, but my will is weak."

I'm sure your date will be happy to hear that. Gotta go. See you tomorrow. 'Bye.

"Bye."

Ellen didn't have "date clothes" and was relieved when Blasingame knocked on her door and she saw he was wearing clean versions of his jeans and shirt that seemed to be his uniform.

He was easy to talk to and Ellen was skilled enough a reporter to see that he was very good at steering the conversation back to her. It was nice to talk about herself to someone – she got the feeling he had studied up on her by reading her Facebook page and published articles and now was trying to find out was the reality was.

On the other hand, she was a reporter and was pretty good, she thought, at getting people to talk about themselves. Slowly, she teased out bits and pieces.

He was born and raised in upper New York state. Graduating from one of the state universities, he started as a contractor but was steadily drawn to restoration work. He travelled a lot, but usually just within the state. Occasionally he went through New England; this was only his second trip to Pennsylvania. He was helping on several projects, including a big one up at Chautauqua, where he and a skilled architect struggled to restore an old home.

He lived alone in a house that, of course, he was restoring. He referred to it as a lesson in humility.

"I want the outside to be as historically accurate as common sense and my bank account will permit but inside, I want every modern convenience I can get. The first thing I built was my office. Polished hardwood floors, paneling with framed photos by people who are really good at it, high speed internet, a big damned desk because I always wanted one." He grinned. "It's my addiction."

She asked about his photography and he smiled again.

"I am still a beginner," Blasingame said. "Everything I learn teaches me I have so much else to learn. I didn't know how ignorant I was until I enrolled in the class."

"I'm a klutz with cameras," Ellen said. "Nothing beyond using my cell. I think I'm awed out of trying by the people who do it professionally."

"What else do you do to keep a balance? Can't work all the time, though I think I violate that periodically."

"Well, I have my friends." She thought of the "Shot to Hell Club." "We get together regularly. Dinner at each other's homes, go out for the evening, that kind of thing."

"They work at the paper?"

"Oh, no. Let's see, one, Hannah, she's a Marine, she's away, back on active duty down at Camp Lejune. Computers. The other, Beth, was in the Army, MP, and works as a police officer for a borough south of here. And Karen is FBI in Philly."

Blasingame glanced at her, his eyebrows climbing.

"Are all your friends proficient in firearms?" His tone was joking.

Ellen smiled.

"They are good people," she said. "I think the NRA would love to use them as poster girls."

"Are you into guns?"

"No, not really," Ellen said slowly. "I've got a permit, taken courses."

"What, you carry a gun?" Blasingame's eyebrows climbed.

"No, not usually," Ellen said. "Farm girl from Ohio, originally my grandfather taught me to shoot. But I don't haul one around regularly."

"As a reporter, I guess you can go into some dangerous places. Probably a good idea to know something about guns."

Ellen nodded; she knew a lot about guns, and the learning had not all come about from courses or her grandfather. "What about you?"

For a moment, Blasingame said nothing as he negotiated a turn into Coalville's square.

"In college, I did a lot of skeet," he said. He turned again and looked for a parking place. "Lot of open space up where I live and I joined a local gun club so I can still do a little of it. Some of those people, they are incredible. It's a sport where people seem to get better with age, so I figure by the time I'm 80 I'll be able to participate in our contests without embarrassing myself."

"Do you ever take your camera to the range?"

"You know, I do," he said. "The club is the only place where any of my pictures are on display. In June, we had the intra-club contests. I was, as usual, pitiful, but I did get, in all modesty, some really nice shots of the contestants."

"Really, how did you do?"

"I came in third." He pulled into a parking place in front of Alfredo's.

"That's not bad."

"It was a field of two."

He shook his head in mock sorrow and Ellen laughed as they got out of the car.

"I feel that way about my photography," she said, stepping onto the sidewalk. "I work every day with real pros, so I've a lot of chances to learn to be humble."

"I know what you mean." He lightly touched Ellen's elbow and they walked toward the restaurant door. "Taking that photography class has really been an education on my tendency to shoot pictures with my eyes closed."

"I can see where that could be problematic," she said with mock seriousness.

This time Blasingame laughed as he held the door open.

Brenda was in the diner going over receipts as Ellen and Blasingame walked into Alfredo's. She voluntarily helped the owner with his bookkeeping to learn about such things, thinking it would help her when she went back to school.

She was a little surprised that it turned out to be, well, *fun*. Getting everything accounted for, making sure the numbers all matched up, was satisfying. It helped, of course, that it really wasn't *her* money, but the owner seemed impressed with how fast she caught on. Now he let her work on "the books," as he called the computer program, without him watching over her shoulder.

Brenda had just tracked down a missing receipt – why didn't he put everything in the same box? – from its perch on a cork bulletin board between the state license and a list of admonishments for employee cleanliness. Probably he had stuck it there as the delivery was completed and then forgot about.

Her phone buzzed and she fished it out of her sweater pocket.

Hey, it's me. It was Carl Johnston, her on again, off again, probably not back on again, with a huge question mark, boyfriend.

"Hey, yourself." She looked out the open door of what passed for an office but the cook was busy, his back to her, and there was no one else.

You seen Fred?

"No." She did not like Fred. When Carl wanted to be mean, he did it with his words. Fred would swing on anyone, which was one reason he never seemed to have a regular girlfriend.

I took the tow out but when I got back, he was gone.

"Going back to his old ways?" Fred had been very large into cocaine and speed in the past and, while he had gotten cleaned up in order to continue working for someone he and Carl called "Mr. Books," she suspected he slipped more than once.

I don't think so. He always locked everything up when he would do that in the past.

"What did Smitty say?" Smitty, Brenda didn't know his real name, worked at the Johnston garage and was generally regarded as good with cars.

He's been out all day, family thing. I called him anyway. Got no idea.

"Me, neither."

All right, you hear anything, you let me know, 'kay? If he comes in, tell him to call me.

"All right."

Brenda broke the connection and frowned. Something wasn't right. Maybe something was going on. There was that guy, asking about the crash and the Johnstons – she had called Carl about it but he had laughed it off. He had sounded a little high, but it might really be nothing, but she knew other people were questioned by the man staying at Willow Run.

No one was supposed to know, but hiding in the floor of her house was a travel bag. In it was a bunch of jewelry, stolen from the crash wreckage. On her dresser was a ring that Carl had given her, a gift for "taking care of things."

She could never wear it. It was stolen. And it had belonged to someone who had died in that terrible accident. She took a long breath, not sure what to do.

Maybe it was all nothing, she tried to tell herself, but she knew, down deep where she could not hide from herself, something was wrong.

Bornstein and Radisson approached the garage carefully; they saw the tow truck parked alongside it and hoped Carl was inside. They parked next to the truck and, for a moment, made no movement and just studied the garage. Radisson kept the air conditioner running; it was very late in the afternoon but the SUV seemed to catch the heat.

"Can't see much," Bornstein said. He glanced around. "I think we're the only customers."

"No time like the present." Radisson shut down the SUV and got out. He slowly looked around. Bornstein eased himself out and stretched, though his eyes kept moving, taking in everything around them.

"Late afternoon, someone might stop by," Bornstein said.

"Keep it casual until we're in his face."

"Just like dear brother Fred."

The two men walked around the front of the garage. The bay doors were down and the office door was locked.

"He's not here," Bornstein said, looking through the glass. He glanced at the office door and the sign hanging inside it. "Poor business man. It's not yet closing time."

"Not hanging around, doing the books or something," Radisson said.

"Not today. Where might he be?"

"Perhaps he's taking care of other business." The two men walked to their dark SUV. "Let me check directory assistance." He tapped at his phone. "Got a street address. Different from Fred's."

"Lovely. Let's see if he is receiving visitors."

Radisson drove as Bornstein supplied navigation. They quickly were on the quiet streets of a residential section of Coalville. He pulled over at Bornstein's direction.

"The white one, that's his house," Bornstein said, glancing at the glowing screen of his phone.

"Looks like no one's home. I don't see any lights."

"Maybe around in back?"

"All right," Radisson said. He pulled away from the curb and went past Carl Johnston's home.

It was a two-story house with a small yard on a street with houses made from three different designs. All had different paint jobs to differentiate them from one another. Carl apparently had liked white with a blue trim. Radisson stopped a few houses down from Carl's. Though the sun was hidden by tree-covered hills, light still came down from the sky.

"Anything in the back of the house?"

"We don't quite have the angle. Not sure. I'll be right back."

Bornstein stepped out of the car and walked back down the street. He went past Carl's and then turned around. A moment later, he was back in the car.

"Light on over the backdoor," he said, "but nothing else."

"I think by now he's noticed brother Fred is missing."

"Fred is dead."

"It's likely he'll be calling mutual friends, going to Fred's hang-outs, that kind of thing."

"And then he'll come home."

"And then he'll come home."

Ellen and Blasingame stayed at Alfredo's longer than she expected. She enjoyed talking with him and encountering his self-deprecating sense of humor. She noticed he never made fun of anyone else, only himself, and often did it, she recognized, as a way of steering away from talking about parts of himself and his history.

Well, that was something she could identify with. Ellen did not readily talk about herself, a trait she had developed as a child. In particular, she did not

64

like to say anything that might be taken as bragging, a value from her grandfather.

She never, however, thought it odd that she was willing to talk about some of the dark experiences she had. Surviving them wasn't about bragging, it was about confronting them, a point a therapist had made. Ellen did not voluntarily talk about that history, believing most people were not equipped to handle it, but Blasingame was a gentle prober, and so it was she briefly talked about the events of the past year when she was stalked and captured by a serial killer.

"That was something you wrote about," Blasingame said. It wasn't a question and Ellen thought he had read her articles.

Writing about that experience was something that she had done not for the momentary and very slight celebrity it provided but to speak for the women who could not. The conversation went there and Blasingame, leaning back in his chair, seemed to follow her closely, nodding as she spoke.

"I think you are right," he said. "We don't hear enough from the people who live through things, especially the hard things. Mostly, we get the summaries of visitors, people who drop into something horrific, do the 'what-when-where-why' and add their opinion and go on to the next thing." He smiled. "I don't mean to offend my dinner partner by disparaging her profession."

"I'm not offended," Ellen said, smiling back. "I think many of us in journalism wrestle with that and other issues. One of the things I like about working online is that we can always update as we learn more, understand more. Hard to do that in television and just about as difficult on the print side."

"You've been at this for a while now. What have you learned that you didn't understand before you got into it?"

"Good question," she said. She paused, considering the question. "I think I did not realize that a good journalist has to have a moral center, a sense of right and wrong, justice, all those things."

"An anchor, you mean? Something to keep you from being swept away by all the ugly things?"

"Yes, certainly. But more than that, more than body armor." Again, Ellen paused. "I found when I go for the story, I am then a part of the story. It affects me, I affect it. I have to take a position. It may not be one shared by any of the people in the story, but, after the 'what-when-where-why,' there's a point when I have to do something, and that decision comes out of my sense of what's right."

"You have to become a participant and lose your objectivity?"

"Not necessarily. Getting the story out may be the best thing to do. The events speak for themselves if people, the right people, learn about them. But, because you are coming from outside the story, you may know something vital, something that might change things. I can give you an example."

"Sure."

"One of our people was in Sub-Saharan Africa doing a story. He talks to people in a village, they've got disease, illness, because they don't have clean water. He files his story, one of dozens, hundreds, just like it. Then he picks up his satellite phone and calls a new friend working in The Water Project, a Christian outfit that works with Africans. They're a nonprofit, he talks about his story, and then suggests a great follow-up would be following The Water Project helping out this particular village. The friend says they are in the middle of a thing with a couple of local NGOs and maybe they can come to the village and use it as a training opportunity. Eventually, they do. He keeps in touch and gets a couple of more stories out of it. And the villager's kids live a little longer because they drink from a well and not a polluted river."

"So, intervening…"

"You intervene by just being there," Ellen said and shook her head. "Justice, if you have a sense of it, means doing what you can with that opportunity. Most of the time, your job is just to get the word out, get the story told. Often, that's enough."

"But sometimes more direct action is needed."

"Sometimes. You can't get a well dug for everyone, there aren't enough dollars, not enough people involved in getting things dug. But if you keep uncovering the need, then maybe the resources fall into place and the wells get dug after all."

"Justice… To be honest, it's not something I would have associated with reporters."

"We're not all blow-dried talking heads who regurgitate the latest emails from various powers that be."

"No, I don't think you are." Blasingame's eyes were level with Ellen's and he did not look away.

"What do you think?" she asked and then immediately wished she could take the question back but it was too late.

"I think," he said slowly, "that justice is at your core, that it influences almost every decision you make." He was not smiling.

"Well," Ellen said, "I'm not a lawyer."

"I'm not talking about the law. Laws come, they go, and they are often inadequate. I'm talking about justice, that sense of right and wrong, that moral center you said you had to have to be a good journalist." He paused, shook his head, and his smile returned. "I am hardly anyone to be judging anyone else."

"It's all right," she said. "I've got some things to think about."

"Don't think too hard," he said, his smile broadening, though his eyes remained serious. "You wouldn't want to talk yourself out of it."

Eventually, they left the restaurant and drove back to Willow Run. They skipped the main cabin and Blasingame walked with Ellen to the door of her cabin. She turned to him expectantly, both excited and anxious about what he might do or not do.

"Thanks for the evening," he said. Lightly his hand touched her elbow.

"And my thanks to you," she said. His hand felt very nice.

He leaned forward and kissed Ellen on the cheek and then leaned back.

"Have a good night," Blasingame said and turned and walked away.

Ellen let herself into her cabin and dropped into a chair and spent the next half hour thinking about what had happened, what had not happened, and whatever the hell it was she wanted.

Day Four

Chapter 4

The morning light promised a clear day as Ellen walked the path to the parking area. As she came abreast of Blasingame's cabin, his door opened and he stepped out, clad as she was in running clothes.

"Good morning," he said.

"Morning. Were you waiting for me?"

"Yes. Is that stalking?"

"I don't think so."

"Besides," he said as he walked beside her, "you're faster than me."

"Really?"

"For any distance at all, I think the entire planet is faster than me."

"How long have you been running?"

"Picked it up in college. My sophomore roommate was Navy ROTC and he got me interested, though I couldn't keep up with him, either."

"Do any competitive runs?"

"Not really. Occasionally a charity 5K, that kind of thing. You?"

"I'm signed up for the Rocky Balboa run in November. 5K."

"Rocky, as in up the steps of the museum?"

"They promise we don't have to run up the steps," she said, smiling. "It's for the Philly Special Olympics. We have a team from the paper."

"Neat. Kind of thing I run in. Have you run 5K?"

"Every Sunday. The rest of the time is just for cardio."

They arrived at the parking lot. Blasingame started running right away, though his pace seemed deliberately slow. Ellen did a few stretches and then started off. She came up on him as he was running back and saw he had picked up his speed. For some reason, she was glad that he had not waited on her and ran his own routine.

As on previous days when she encountered him running, Blasingame finished before her. As she slowed down to a walk around the parking area, she spotted him to one side on a path into the trees. He was partially hidden and she paused to watch him. With his t-shirt lying to one side, he was doing

69

push-ups on the earth and even from a distance she could see the broad slabs of muscles in his back working.

Ellen watched for a moment, enjoying the view. Then something changed. Blasingame kept rising and falling, rising and falling, each repetition perfect. He did not sag or slow down. It was like watching a machine. He held himself rigidly – even the muscles in his legs stood out. And still he did not stop.

He was not exercising casually; he was not a casual athlete. She was reminded of the first time she saw one of the Philadelphia Eagles' wide receivers exercising – Blasingame was like a professional.

His repetitions slowed but his body remained rigid. He seemed to fight to force another, then another. The last one had him pushing his body away from the earth with a trembling exertion but he did not quit. When he got to the top of the movement, Ellen expected him to stop. He did not.

Blasingame slowly lowered himself, a movement that seemed to make his body vibrate. Then, incredibly, he pushed himself upward. When he was half way up, he stopped. He was not pausing; his body shook as he tried to force himself the rest of the way.

Finally, he stopped. Blasingame did not let himself fall to the ground. He eased down until his bare chest was on the path. Almost immediately he stood and brushed off his front, his back still towards Ellen.

He reached down and picked up his t-shirt. He turned and saw Ellen.

Another man looked at her. This was not Bob Blasingame of the gentle smile. The hard eyes and grim face she saw belonged to someone else, a fighter. His push-ups, she realized, were not for her benefit, it wasn't showing off, but some kind of battle with himself.

Something like what she did, she realized, but more… Was 'ferocious' the word?

Then she blinked and it was Blasingame again. He smiled, looking a little embarrassed as he waved at her.

"How's it going?" he said, raising his voice.

"Not too bad. You really push yourself."

"Only because I'm usually slothful." He pulled his t-shirt on and walked towards her. "I really, really hate exercising."

"I can identify with that."

He was now in front of her. His sweat made the t-shirt cling to his torso, revealing the muscles beneath.

"Do you do anything besides running?"

"Back in Philly I take instruction in fighting."

"Judo, a self-defense course, something like that?"

"Not self-defense," she said. The two of them walked towards their cabins. "I mean, yes, it's used for self-defense but it's mostly about how to attack back. Bunch of techniques."

"Not chasing after a black belt, then?"

"No," she said, feeling a little embarrassed. "It's more 'real world' than that."

"I have a taekwondo instructor who would argue about that with you but I know what you mean."

"Well, fighting is just something you do while you reload."

"I don't think you're getting the spiritual aspect of the martial arts."

They came up on Blasingame's cabin.

"See you at breakfast?" he asked as he turned to it.

"Yes. I'm taking my camera up into the woods later."

"I still have some places in town to check out."

"Not much of a vacation for you, if you have to keep working."

"You're right," he said from his doorway, smiling. "But this is me relaxing – you ought to see me when I'm really working."

She smiled and continued on to her own cabin.

Ellen beat Blasingame back to the dining room. The family was gone but Steve and Thomas were there, working on large omelets. Joyce smiled and waved.

"Saw you running," Joyce said. "You need pancakes. And an omelet."

"Try the one with cilantro," Steve said, circling his plate with his fork. "It's incredible."

"Cilantro is our friend," Joyce said. "Want to give it a try?"

"All right, yes," Ellen said. "Don't know if I'll finish it. They look large."

"No hill for a real climber," Joyce said. "I'll make a…"

"Short stack!" Steve and Thomas said together and laughed. Ellen smiled as she went for coffee, not sure what the joke was.

Ellen sat down and another couple, a gray-haired man who looked like a professor and a slightly gray-haired woman who looked even more like one, came in. Greetings were exchanged and Joyce tried to talk them into omelets but both settled on pancakes and "a little bacon." Steve and Thomas grinned at each other; Ellen still had not figured out the joke.

Blasingame came in and headed immediately to the coffee.

"I may live after all," he said as he took his first sip.

"Pancakes and omelets to order," Joyce said.

"Absolutely," Blasingame said. "I'll try a cheese omelet."

"Try it with cilantro."

"All right, I will." He looked at Steve and Thomas. "Is she still trying to murder us by pancake?"

"By short stack," Steve said and all three men laughed. Joyce waved at them dismissively and grinned.

"What's the joke?" Ellen asked as Blasingame sat across from her.

"The other day…" His voice trailed off and he watched Joyce approach. "You'll see."

Joyce's version of a "short stack" of pancakes was two, but two that were massive. In total bulk, they were probably the same as three, maybe four, regular pancakes. Coupled with the large omelet, Ellen thought she would never finish it all.

"Patti said the other night," Blasingame said, "Joyce was going to kill someone one of these days with her pancakes. We've been joking about it ever since."

"They are huge." It turned out they were also delicious. Ellen concentrated on the omelet – cilantro *was* our friend, she decided – but ate almost all of the pancakes.

"I don't know where I found the room," she said.

"Hollow leg?" Blasingame asked, smiling. "That's my excuse."

"I may borrow it. Are you off now?" She waved to Steve and Thomas as they left and Thomas winked.

"Yes," he said. "There's a fellow just east of town specializing in German work. Wrought iron, tables and chairs, long rifles, and I want to take a look. Those German immigrants to this end of Pennsylvania did some great work and I have a client who might be interested in getting some things for a tavern he's building."

"Including long rifles?"

"This was the place for them."

"Back home, we called them Kentucky long rifles."

"They started here," Blasingame said. "German gunsmiths set up shop here, Germantown. Made a new weapon, one people took to Kentucky."

"I've heard that. I need to spend more time on the internet, catch up on my local history."

"Google is our friend," Blasingame said, smiling. "You can learn a lot on the internet."

"I'm trying to avoid the temptation while on vacation. I start hitting my news sites and then I'm looking at our site and then my head's back at work."

"Technology is not our friend, then?"

"I myself am going back to papyrus."

"I better be rolling," Blasingame said. He stood up. "Spending the day in the forest?"

"Meeting a friend for lunch."

"Try not to outrun the deer," Blasingame said. "It makes them feel bad." Then he was gone. Joyce came over and gathered the dishes.

"I knew you could do it," she said, walking into the kitchen.

"I couldn't help myself. The pancakes were delicious."

"They've been a hit." She paused. "You trying for some photos?"

"No competition for your other guests."

"Well, when you come to the fork, bear left and then right. It's a big circle and will bring you back here. There's a spot on the side of a hill and you can see almost all the way to Coalville. Pretty place. Might get some good pictures there."

"Thanks. I'll check it out."

"He's in pretty good shape," Joyce said, coming back to do more clearing. "He reminds me of Patti's brother."

"Athlete?"

"SEAL. Not all buff and ripped. Not Arnold. But muscles that get used."

"Reminded me of some Eagles I saw work out."

"Yes, like them." She paused, balancing plates. "Someone you might want on your side."

"Well, he's a contractor."

"They all say that," Joyce said as she walked back to the kitchen.

Ellen sipped her coffee for a while.

They all say that.

The real estate agent's name was Debbie Wheeler and she was happy. Chester County had been in a slump for house sales for what felt like a hundred years but was finally coming back to life. Better than that, she had a couple, newlyweds, eager to find a place in the country. Well, Chester County had country, if you wanted it.

Debbie slowed to halt at a stop sign and checked for traffic. There wasn't any on these back roads, other than the occasional school bus, but she didn't want her clients to die a fiery death in mangled metal until after she got her commission. And definitely not in her four-year old Cadillac Escalade. She looked in her rearview mirror; the couple were looking in all directions at once, obviously enthralled with not being in a city. She noticed they were still holding hands.

She tried to tell herself that they would lose that and their enchantment with the rural countryside of northern Chester County but she couldn't maintain her cynicism. Just because she was divorced…

Keep holding onto one another, you two. That's the secret.

That, and not letting cocaine become more important than your wife and son.

Debbie re-focused on driving and turned onto the road.

"Less than a mile from here," she said. "We'll go a little bit north and then turn west."

"What happened there?" the woman asked.

"Looks like there was a fire," the man said.

"That plane crash last month," Debbie said.

"That's a shame."

"Yes, it was. Over there on the right, you can just see that pasture. That's one of your neighbors. Dairy farm."

"Cows," the man said.

"That's nice," the woman said.

"Most of the country around here is like that," Debbie explained. "Farms, some dairy, some crops like corn. This has been a good year for corn. And large wooded areas. Here's our turn. Now, straight ahead, that road curves to the west and goes past some state game lands. They're right next to a state park. Very pretty place. Good for picnicking. To the right, that other road picks up a state route that will take you to the turnpike if you are in a hurry to go someplace." She made her turn to the left.

"You wanted some privacy," Debbie said. "Not a lot of houses down this road. Your place is on the left. Across from it, that's a neighboring farm and, as you can see, it's all wood lots next to the road. Deer are active around here."

"Deer," the woman said.

"There it is," the man said.

As they approached, what they saw first was a break in the trees and then the break resolved itself into a driveway going back to a house with a porch. Off to one side was a metal barn about a story and a half high. Debbie parked in front of the house.

"It looks beautiful," the woman said as she opened her door and Debbie smiled. With couples, you sold homes to the wife first.

"It's been kept up," Debbie said. "They kept it off the market because no one's been buying. But the family has had regular maintenance performed, furnace checks, plumbing, all that. We have the records."

"Good," the man said.

"Do you want to see the house first or the barn? I know you wanted an outside building…"

"For my pottery," she said. "Yes, let's take a quick look at the barn and then we can take our time in the house."

"Good idea," Debbie said. She had the information memorized but she consulted her tablet anyway. "It's a pole barn, concrete floor."

"What's a 'pole barn'?" the man asked.

"Generally, it doesn't use a heavy-duty foundation," Debbie said. "Wooden supports frame it and steel sheets make the sides and roof. Generally cheaper to build than all-wood construction."

"I see."

"There are roller doors at both ends and a regular door at this end, as you can see. And I have the key for the padlock if you want to try the rollers."

"I think the door will work," the woman said, reaching for the knob.

"It's wired but if you want higher voltage, you'll want…"

"Is that man dead?"

Sergeant Peterson stood outside the barn and watched as the Highway Patrol cruiser arrived and pulled in next to the ambulance. The county deputy, a young woman with less than a year in the sheriff's service, licked her lips. She had held it together when she went into the barn and handled all the county coordination, but needed to catch her breath. Peterson, having seen Johnston, did not begrudge her that need.

"Deputy," he said, "could you do me a favor and check with your dispatcher that my fire police have closed off the roads? I heard them say they were at the east intersection but I'm not sure the folks over on the west side are in place."

"Not a problem," she said. "We had deputies at both intersections but I heard the east car get released, so, yeah, your people are there, but I'll call in about the west one. You want to brief the trooper?" She seemed to relax a little, now that she had something to do besides stand next to a metal barn with a dead man sitting inside.

"Sure, no problem." He nodded and she walked over to her SUV.

Peterson raised a hand for the trooper and got a nod back from the gray-clad figure.

"Michaels," the trooper said as an introduction. He held out his hand.

"Peterson, Coalville PD." Peterson shook his hand.

"What have we got?" the trooper asked.

"Male, Caucasian, by the name of Fred Johnston. Owns and operates a garage in Coalville." He paused as the trooper took notes – were cops born with memo pads in their left shirt pocket?

"Apparent cause?" It would be 'apparent' until a medical examiner determined the official, actual cause of death.

"Suffocation. He was tied to a chair and a plastic bag was put over his head."

"Shit."

"Indeed. He has a file with us and county. Drugs, mostly. Theft, some trafficking, likely. Used to work a lot for Tallman, not so much for the new guy."

"Connection to the house cleaning?" A year before, Tallman's chief lieutenant died in a parking lot trying to take down an FBI agent and Tallman himself later was found in a shallow grave with two significant holes in his head; someone new was running things in Chester County.

"Your guess is as good as mine," Peterson said, "but I don't think so. Things have been very quiet over the past several months. We think a guy named Books has taken over but he's personally been very low profile." He grimaced. "We've got fee-bee leading a task force in town, something about the air crash, and they're going to love this."

"My sympathy," Michaels said. "So, county has this?"

"For the moment. I was first responder and we have Coalville fire police at the intersections east and west of here."

"Saw them on the way in." It was not unusual in Pennsylvania counties to have the local volunteer fire police – people who usually directed traffic away from firefighters – pressed into service to do the same service for accidents and police calls.

"The deputy came next and we'll get some more rollers from the county sheriff's service in the next few minutes. Nature of the crime, I figure they will bring in the state. Maybe the feds if this is related." He grimaced. "Did I mention we have a task force in town?"

"Life can be hard."

Peterson snorted a half-laugh and the trooper grinned.

"I saw the deputy." He put away his notepad. "She handling it for the county?"

"She is." Peterson nodded and smiled slightly. "Swallowing hard to hold it down but she did and took care of the protocol boxes."

"Well, good for her. I'll get on the horn and see what the deal is." He nodded to one side. "Those the people who found it?"

"Affirmative. Real estate agent and the people she was showing around. I've gotten a prelim from them. Not much. Opened the door, saw the man, stepped back and hit nine-one-one."

Michaels shook his head and put away his pad. Peterson looked up at the blue sky.

"Nice day," he said.

"Yep," Michaels said. "Now watch some son of a bitch screw it up."

Peterson chuckled as he watched the trooper walk back to his cruiser.

Ellen enjoyed her hike through the trees so much she almost was late meeting Karen Deevers for lunch. She entered the diner and saw Karen sitting in a booth to one side, sitting so she could watch the door. She always did.

Ellen had not met Karen when their paths crossed in Ohio in 1994 but the older woman, 26 at that time while Ellen was 13, appeared to be far less than the thirteen years that separated them. Karen was of average height with an oval, inquisitive face that could look amused or intimidating, depending on the situation. She wore her naturally blond hair short and the silver threads in it were hard to spot. Her eyes, whatever the expression on the rest of her face, were almost always intent, carefully studying whatever, or whomever, was in front of her.

She had met her husband, James "JJ" Jeffers, in Ohio when he was a county deputy sheriff. They went through a rough patch after JJ left law enforcement to become a lawyer, but they straightened things out in spite of, maybe in part because of, Karen taking down a pair of killers outside a pizza restaurant.

It had not been the first time she killed someone and was why she sat with her back to the wall so she could see whoever came through the diner's door.

"Hey, lady," Ellen said and slid into the booth.

"Hey, yourself," Karen said, grinning. She mocked a toast with her iced tea.

"How goes it?" Ellen asked as Karen slid a menu over.

"Keeping busy. Talked to JJ this morning and he said to say 'hi' and remind you of the cookout next month."

"It's in my calendar," Ellen said, "which I have managed not to look at even once since going on vacation."

"Not paying much attention to your phone, either."

"Sorry about that," Ellen said, with no trace of contrition in her voice. She smiled as she studied the list of salads. "I've kept it on most of the time but I've ignored the damned thing."

"So, you're not working?"

"Are you about to show me your ID?" Ellen cocked her head to one side. "And might I ask why Special Agent Karen Deevers of the Philadelphia FBI office is here in charming Coalville?"

"You may not. But, really, are you working?"

"No. Cross my heart."

"Good." She paused. "Let's order; I'm starving."

Karen waved to the waitress and it turned out to be Brenda.

"Hey, how are you doing?" Brenda asked as she walked up to their table and took out her order pad. "How's the vacation?"

"See?" Ellen said to Karen. "I'm on vacation." She looked up at Brenda. "It's wonderful. Did I tell you about the deer?"

"No."

"Ran right by them." She nodded at Karen. "This is my friend Karen. We go back years. And this is Brenda."

"Glad to meet you," Brenda said. "Are you on vacation, too?"

"And you. No, working, unfortunately. Pretty part of the county."

"Yes, it is, if you really, *really* like farms and trees."

"Brenda is looking at going to nursing school."

"Cool," Karen said. "Good nurses are worth their weight in gold. What do you recommend for lunch?"

"Well," Brenda said, "Ellen's going for a salad, I'm betting, because they filled her up this morning at Willow Run..."

"She really did," Ellen agreed. "Yes to the salad, please. The Greek, I think."

"Do you feel like a sandwich?" Brenda asked, turning to Karen. "The pastrami is deli-style with a real rye bread."

"I'll do it."

"Chips?"

"No, no side."

Ellen ordered an iced tea and Brenda went off.

"So why are you here?" Ellen asked.

"Off the record," Karen said. "No attribution. You get first shot if this turns into anything."

"Agreed."

"The plane crash."

"You are investigating it?"

"No, no. NTSB is on top of that, looks to be mechanical failure. No, we're acting on a tip. A CI told us something was being transported from Philly to Harrisburg to go on to Albany. NTSB didn't find it. It may have been stolen from the crash site."

"Harrisburg? Long way to Albany."

"That's one point."

"And who was it for?"

Karen shook her head.

"Maybe it was destroyed in the crash and fire."

"No. Carry-ons and checked luggage were clear of the fire."

"But stolen?"

"Here's how it is after a crash. NTSB is very, very thorough. Every piece of luggage, and I mean down to iPods, is inspected, checked, even weighed. Even with nametags and bar strips on them, luggage can take a month or more before it is released to survivors. More complicated for next of kin, of course, but they try to keep the paperwork harassment down. Right now, they are dragging their feet letting anything go."

"But, again, stolen?"

"The crash was marked by a large number of locals arriving at the site, some even before law enforcement and emergency services got there." She took a breath. "A number of things are missing."

"I see." Ellen was silent for a moment, thinking of the coverage given to the volunteers who had helped at the site, assisting in putting out the fires and locating bodies. *There is always one...*

"So what is missing?"

"Identified items include three watches, some rings, and some carry-on bags were forced open, not from crash impact. We think jewelry from them was taken but the next of kin are still doing an inventory."

"Is that what your CI said was being shipped?"

"We're not talking about what it was," Karen said. "But it was not personal items. It was, let's say it was payment. Maybe like a gift. From one baddie to another."

"Money?"

"We're not talking."

"It wasn't drugs."

Karen smiled.

"And how do you know that, ace reporter?"

"No mule would be dumb enough to try to carry a bag full of drugs onto an airplane while walking through security."

"Other ways to carry things without people seeing or sniffer dogs noticing."

"And there are no DEA people with you in Coalville."

"How the hell did you know that?"

"Didn't, until just now." Ellen pointed at herself. "Ace reporter, remember?"

"No comment." Karen paused. "All right, here's another piece. We are not sure what it is. Could be cash, negotiable securities, the Hope Diamond, the Maltese Falcon, we don't know." She grimaced. "

"A mystery. How do you know it got onto the airplane?"

"There isn't any missing checked baggage, so we had the same question. To complicate things, we don't know who took it onto the airplane."

"Video...?"

"Camera covering the gate broke." She shook her head. "Sometimes the bad guys catch a break. We have people going through all the other terminal tapes but we're not having a lot of luck because we're not sure what we're looking for."

"Got to the tapes late and the loops expired?"

"Very good, padawan. But we are the FBI..."

"So, you are trying to recover the video from the surveillance system that's been overwritten a dozen times?"

"Closer to twenty. Our tech people are pretty certain it is impossible. We're checking them all anyway, just in case."

"Who was carrying it?"

"That's the other delightful piece of missing information." She sipped her tea. "We don't know. They brought it through security, whatever it was, but no one recalls seeing anything unusual, like a brick of gold-plated cocaine or whatever."

"Good grief."

Both women paused as their lunch arrived. After they ate for a moment, Ellen looked up.

"But there's no luggage missing?"

"Well… Every piece of checked luggage or carry-on bags described by next of kin has been accounted for, but it might have been inside the someone's bag."

"You can't track the bag itself but maybe you don't have to."

"Do go on."

"You are here checking the volunteers at the crash site, seeing if you can find out who stole the missing things that the relatives alerted you to. And, whoever that person was, it might likely be that same person took whatever the thing going to Albany was."

Karen touched her own nose but didn't say anything.

"Well, that's going to mean a lot of leg work, checking on everyone who was there."

"More than that," Karen said, wiping some mustard from her lips. She said nothing else and just looked at Ellen.

"Oh, hell," Ellen said, her voice low as she leaned forward, "you think whoever the thing belongs to is going to be looking. You're here for the bad guy."

Before Karen responded, a low, rapid bell announced her cell phone. She reached into her coat pocket and brought it to her ear.

"Deevers."

She remained silent and then nodded.

"I'll be waiting outside," she said and put the phone away. She looked at Ellen. "I've got to go."

"I've got this."

"Don't go poking around," Karen said as she slid from the booth. "I'll keep you in the loop as much as I can."

"Can I ask what's going on?"

Karen wiped her mouth and put the napkin on the table. As she leaned forward, her coat opened enough that Ellen could see her holstered .40-caliber Glock.

"I think your bad guy is here," Karen quietly said and then she was gone.

The police car that picked up Karen outside the diner only had its flashers on until it was nearly out of town and Ellen heard the new-borne siren gradually fade into the distance.

Brenda came up after a moment and looked at Karen's plate.

"She didn't like her sandwich?"

"I think she liked it but she was called away."

"I saw her take a call. Do you want me to box it and you can hold onto it for her?"

"No – I don't know when she'll get free. Besides, I'd probably eat it for dinner anyway."

Brenda smiled as she picked up Karen's plate and took it away. She came back and nodded toward the window.

"Is that your CR-V?"

"Yes."

"Is it as reliable as they say? I'm thinking about getting one."

"Mine's been anvil-reliable," Ellen said. "Had it for a year now. Got it used. What are you driving?"

"Doctor Frankenstein's creature's car. I call it my 'Frankencar.'"

"That sounds terrible."

"Actually, it's been all right, for a nine-year-old Toyota. My ex-boyfriend brought it back to life after the insurance company declared it totaled. He got it from the old owner for the loose change he found under his couch cushions and then sold it to me for less than his labor would have run. But it's got parts from a couple of different manufacturers, its paint looks like something mothers use to scare their kids into going to bed, and the only place I can get it inspected is at his garage."

Ellen chuckled.

"I only drive it to work," Brenda said. "Fortunately, that's only a couple of miles, right off of Stanford."

"I came in on Stanford Avenue, I think. Pretty houses."

"They're old but used to belong to the people with money, the coal mine owners. I live a few miles further, actually where it's just the county road. You may have passed me. Out in the country."

"I remember seeing a lot of corn."

"That's my yard," she said, smiling. "I have corn all around me this year."

"I saw a couple of houses on the way in, one with a barn."

"That's the farmer who does all the corn. You probably didn't see my house. The drive loops in and out, so I'm far enough back that the trees block the view of it."

"The bright red mailbox?"

"That's it. I'm surprised you remember that."

"Back home, Ohio, we always gave directions using mailboxes. 'Go down the road, look for the milk can mailbox, take the next right,' that kind of thing."

"Country girl. Well, it's a pretty straight route to get there from here. I think Frankencar is used to simple directions. If it was complicated to get there and back, if I were to open a road atlas in front of it, the poor thing would have a heart attack."

Ellen chuckled. "Sounds like an interesting car."

"When you leave, just look around the diner. It's in the little side parking slots we use. You won't mistake it for anyone else's."

"I will. Lucky your boyfriend owns a garage."

"Owns it with his brother," she said and the humor that had lightened her voice was gone. "And he's more my ex- than current."

"Ah."

"But he's a good mechanic. Everyone says so. Has a natural talent in that direction."

"Being an 'ex' might make business a little awkward."

"Well, we've managed to still stay friends, I think."

"That's an achievement. Things don't always work out like that when people break up."

"Well, it hasn't been totally smooth. I can't say that. His brother was pretty obnoxious and he could be nasty himself but, still…" She let her voice trail off. "Sorry for bending your ear like this."

"Not a problem at all." Ellen smiled. "And I will take a look at your Frankenstein car."

Brenda smiled and walked to another booth to take an order.

Ellen, having said she would, went around back to see the Frankencar. On the outside, it was odd with the doors on the driver's side being two different colors, neither of which matched the hood. Inside, it looked like the rear seat was covered by a different colored fabric than the front seats. Dents and ripples were liberally distributed over the whole car. She shook her head; she had thought she had driven a real junker when she was in college but Brenda's car had it beat.

Frankencar. Ellen was still smiling when she drove away in her own car.

Bornstein and Radisson saw Carl Johnston pull into the garage but the morning traffic and early business kept them from attempting to approach him. They were sipping coffee when Sergeant Peterson passed them, siren and flashers on, heading north.

"Someone's had an accident," Bornstein said tentatively.

"Morning commuters," Radisson replied, nodding. "Probably late for work and pushing it."

"It is a little late to be going to work." He shook his head. "People just don't plan ahead."

"I hate commuter traffic."

"Well, we won't have to put up with that shit much longer."

His partner raised his cardboard cup of coffee in a toast of agreement. Neither knew Peterson was responding to the call from the real estate agent.

When the second police car, this one ferrying Special Agent Karen Deevers, sped past twenty minutes later, Radisson shook his head.

"No fire vehicles, no ambulances," he said. "I hate to be a pessimist, but I think someone looked inside our barn."

"Dammit."

"Yeah." He took the last sip. "They'll probably be coming back here to notify young Carl of his brother's demise."

Bornstein said nothing, but frowned as he started the car. Just to check, he drove towards the farm but the turn onto the road they had used was now blocked by a police vehicle and a county deputy. He made a small wave to the officer but kept going north.

"Well, that's a lousy way to start the day," he said after a moment.

"Yeah. Still better than Carl's."

"True. I'm going to circle east and go on back to Coalville."

"All right."

Blasingame was admiring a collection of long barreled flintlock rifles when he heard the distant siren of a police car.

"Fire?" he said to the middle-aged man who owned the story.

"Don't think so," the man replied. "You'd hear the siren go at the fire station calling people in first. That's a police car."

"I see." Blasingame nodded. "These are beautiful."

"They really are. Now the one at the bottom, that's had a major change. Late in its life, it was updated to percussion cap. The previous owner had it changed back to flintlock, using a modern kit. But he saved the old percussion gear. I'm having it restored to its percussion set-up."

"That's, what?, 40-caliber?"

"Yes. Good eye. Of course, a lot of Pennsylvania rifles became percussions as they were handed down over the generations but those three above it were all maintained as flintlocks."

"Can I take a picture? I have a client who might be interested in all three, maybe all four."

"Sure. Do you need more light?"

"It's got a flash."

Blasingame took a picture and then checked his phone. He nodded.

"Got it." He looked up. "You said you had a table with inlay work?"

"Sure do. It's over there. Let me show you."

Blasingame followed the man who kept up a steady stream of descriptions of almost every table, chair, whatever, that they passed.

They were examining the table when they heard the second police car, the one taking Karen Deevers to the barn holding a suffocated Fred Johnston.

"Not good," the man said. He crouched and pointed at one of the legs. "You see what they did here? That's all original."

Blasingame squatted down and nodded silently. He did not appear to be interested in the fading sound of the police car.

Karen Deevers looked at the slumped body of Fred Johnston, White male, 37, five feet, eleven, two-fifty, multiple prior arrests, two incarcerations, and frowned.

"The county medical examiner is on his way," Sergeant Peterson said. He had been told to provide the Fee-Bee with anything she wanted; that was how task forces worked when the feds were involved. Automatically they went to the top, like, he thought, other things that float.

"Do you know this guy? I mean, beyond the briefing I got on the drive over."

The question did not surprise Peterson. First, because Deevers did not seem to have a hair up her butt about being an FBI agent and was willing to ask questions of the local police. Second, because cops from outside his jurisdiction routinely thought the local police knew everyone. In the case of Fred Johnston, it happened to be true.

"Yes. Long history of being an asshole, but a low-level one. Petty stuff growing up. We had some people not related to him also named Johnston near here involved in a bunch of thefts and murders, they made it into a movie, and I think he felt it was a calling from God, last name and all."

"Seriously?"

"Movie came out in the mid-'80s, he was only nine or ten or so but, so the story goes, he got a copy of it in '97 and it was a turning point in his life."

"I remember. Walken, Penn. 'In Close Range,' I think."

"'*At* Close Range,'" Peterson said. "Close enough for government work."

That got a smile from Deevers.

"Had a good song in it by Madonna. I was a fan."

"Your secret is safe with me. Anyway, Fred tried to break into the big time but they, the people who organize things in the county, used him only as a utility player. He moved small shipments of drugs for them, mostly meth, from here into Philly and west to Harrisburg. He went to jail for car theft and then got nailed again for possession. He brought his brother Carl into his business. He runs, ran, a garage on the edge of town."

"Got it," Deevers said. She had stopped studying Johnston and folded her arms. "He was on your list."

"You read it?" This time Peterson was surprised.

"Yes. He and his brother both were on it. We didn't get a chance to get your written file on him but he was there because he was a small fish?"

"Mostly, because of proximity and, yeah, a fish. He and his brother were some of the first at the crash scene. When NTSB said relatives were reporting stuff missing, those two would be on the list, but when you guys said something important had disappeared, oh, yeah, stealing from the dead, that's Fred's speed."

"But he wasn't in the big leagues?"

"Not full time. One thing was, he used pretty heavily. Went into rehab, hell, must have been four or five times. Untrustworthy."

Deevers nodded and her eyes returned to Johnston's slumped form.

"If we find a connection to the crash, maybe someone else thought he was good for it."

"Thought occurred to me." Peterson paused. "Met a man a few days ago. He visited the crash. Claimed he knew only a little about it but had some details that suggested he knew more than that. Had done some homework, you know? Robert Blasingame, nothing on file. He's on vacation but doing a little shopping in our antique stores."

"Antiques can be an addiction, they tell me. Visiting from where?"

"New York."

"I think a box just got ticked. Where is he?"

"He's staying at Willow Run Bed and Breakfast, just west of…"

"I know it," Deevers said and shook her head. "I have a friend staying there."

"Well, well."

"And the friend is a reporter."

"Told someone earlier that somebody would screw up what was otherwise a nice day."

"She isn't working, really on vacation."

"Hell of a coincidence."

"Sometimes that's how it is. This," she nodded at the body, "was done by someone who likes pain."

"What do you mean?"

"Whoever it was, maybe they had questions for Fred, same kinds of questions we might have had."

"Looking for the bag or whatever?"

"Thought Fred was good for it. Asks questions. Bag over the head, that's painful. Gets the answers but doesn't cap him, not going for the quick kill. Puts the bag over his head one last time and then stands here and watches."

"Had to wait to be sure." He nodded. "Cruel. No reason he couldn't just shoot him in the head and be on his way. Sure, he had to have a gun. Fred would not be cooperative without one stuck in his ear." Peterson raised his eyebrows. "Your friend has no idea who might be having breakfast with her?"

"I'd like to move on Blasingame, one way or the other, pretty quickly." She paused. "All right, he's from New York, we think the thing involves New York, and he's been to the crash site. You ran him, I gather."

"Yes," Peterson said. "Just local at first but we went national. Came back totally clean."

"Let me see if I can turn up anything." She paused again. "Whoever did this, he had a reason. If he's looking for the missing bag, he learned something about Johnston that brought them together. Maybe he was asking questions and someone said Johnston was at the crash site."

"I can check around town. I've seen his car at a few shops, we'll talk to the people."

"Be interesting to hear what he talked about with them."

Several hours later, Ellen emerged from the forest cradling Willow Run, studying her camera's display. The battery needed recharging. She smiled – she had remembered to bring the camera battery charger but had forgotten her cell's charger. Well, one was more important than the other.

As she looked up, she saw a Coalville dark blue SUV in the parking area. Robert Blasingame and a uniformed police officer were talking in front of it. Surprisingly, so was Karen Deevers.

She kept walking towards the group. Blasingame noticed her first, raising his eyebrows, a small smile on his face. Deevers, looking where Blasingame looked, had a very serious expression as she made a slight negative shake of her head.

Before Ellen could decide what Deevers was trying to tell her, Blasingame took a step towards her and spoke across the parking lot.

"I have to go into town," Blasingame said. "They have a few questions for me. It won't take long. I know it's awkward, but would you like to join me for dinner?"

"Join me," Ellen said, "if you're free. I'll be at Alfredo's at six thirty."

Blasingame laughed and Deevers looked like she was moving from serious to angry – the police officer, a clipboard in his left hand, remained impassive.

"I think I'll make it," he said. "Thank you." He turned back to the others as Ellen turned onto the path to her cabin.

What was going on?

The Coalville Police Department occupied a two-story stone building that was well over a hundred years old. After the Vietnam War, a wooden extension was built off the back. The flood of federal money after 9/11 had not been used to purchase armored vehicles but to upgrade communications and computers, add to the training budget, and remodel two interrogation rooms. A space between them now was a small room from which observers could watch and listen while cameras recorded conversations.

The Coalville PD Chief, an older white man with gray hair cut military-short named Jerry Davis, was in the small room watching as Blasingame came into Interrogation Room One. He was followed immediately by one of the CPD officers and then Special Agent Karen Deevers. Sergeant Peterson was out at the front desk, talking to the covering officer, having spent the past several hours talking to shop owners about Blasingame. Davis understood the business of the missing bag was federal, so Deevers would do the questioning.

That was why he was surprised when Peterson stepped into the room almost immediately after Deevers and Blasingame sat down. He motioned to Deevers and the FBI agent followed him out as if having the start of questioning a potential murderer interrupted was the most common thing in the world. Davis joined them in the hall.

"We have something," Peterson said. "Fred Johnston and his brother Carl stole something from the crash site. We have a witness. She just came in. And," he motioned with his head, "Blasingame asked almost everyone in town about the crash and who got there first. I found several antique dealers who he talked to about it."

"No shit," Davis said. His twelve years in the Marine Corps had left some rough edges around his use of language, something that twenty-three years as a police officer had done nothing to smooth.

"Did anyone tell him the Johnstons were there?" Deevers leaned towards Peterson slightly, anticipating the answer.

"Almost everyone. And the witness, Brenda Cassidy, works at the diner, says they got there almost immediately and stole a bag and things. She's turned it in. Jewelry. They hid it in her house."

"In her house?" Davis was doubtful.

"Carl built some hiding places in it when he remodeled her house. They were close, almost engaged. He used the house to hide stuff he and his brother were moving. Probably drugs but she hasn't gotten into any details about that and I haven't pushed. But nothing for the past year."

"Why not?"

"They broke up. Her choice. She says they managed to remain friends. She says Fred and Carl stole from the crash and hid jewelry in one of the hideaways and claims she found it by accident. Didn't know it was there, didn't know Carl still had a key to her house."

"Why is she coming forth now?"

"She's heard about Fred. That brought her in."

"All right," Deevers said, nodding. "We still don't know what they were moving. Our CI, as I said yesterday, wasn't specific, so it could be jewelry. We need some answers from Blasingame. Nice work."

"Thanks."

"You said she brought the jewelry in?"

"Affirmative."

"Let's talk with her before Blasingame; she may be our trump card to play."

"Got it," Peterson said. "I'll put her in the other room." He turned away and walked down the hall.

"This looks good," Davis said. "Do you have the ME prelim on Fred?"

"Yes, thanks. Critical part is the time of death."

"Late afternoon yesterday, maybe 4 PM, more or less."

Deevers did not reply. Coming down the hall was Sergeant Peterson and Brenda Cassidy. The young woman's eyes were red-rimmed from crying. Davis nodded at her and opened the door to Interrogation Room Two. After he closed it, he turned to Deevers.

"I'll let Blasingame know you'll be back in a few minutes. Won't hurt him to stir in his own juices for a bit."

"Nice thought." Deevers went into the room and took a seat next to Peterson.

Brenda had a tissue and, though she was not crying, dapped at her eyes. On the table was a dark leather bag, rigid from an internal metal frame, and small, perhaps no more than eight inches in length. Beneath a gold clasp, the bag had been embossed with the letter *M*. It opened easily and Deevers saw it had numerous pieces of jewelry, including rings, earrings, a pearl necklace, and several bracelets. Oddly, there were several watches, some obviously men's.

Deevers did not regard herself as an expert on the arcane art of jewelry appraisal but none of the pieces seemed particularly valuable – there was nothing like the Hope Diamond leaping into view. She took all the pieces out and carefully arranged them on the tabletop. Handling them did nothing to dispute her first impression. Some of what she laid out belonged to men, though most were women's. She looked at Brenda.

"I want to change my story," Brenda said. "Can I do that?" Her tissue now had something to do as a pair of tears went down her face.

"Go ahead."

"I said I didn't know the bag was in my house. That wasn't true." She took a deep breath. "Is it all right if I start at the beginning?"

"Yes."

"Carl and I, we were pretty close. He moved in with me. You know he mostly works as a mechanic in Fred's garage. He does carpentry on the side. He's done work around town for people. Pretty good at it, everyone says. Anyway, while he was with me, he did a lot of work on my house. When he did, he also made these hiding places. A couple in the floor, two in the wall behind the paneling, that kind of thing. It was a game with him, you know? He'd tell me, I'd look, and, when I couldn't find it, he'd show me. He always said there were other hiding places but after we broke up, I didn't ask him where they were. Anyway, I told Officer Peterson that he put the bag in my house without my knowing. That wasn't true." More tears ran down her face, pursued by the tissue.

"You knew they took something?"

Brenda nodded.

"We were at the crash. I rode in their truck. I thought we were going to help someone, something like that."

"You were with the Johnston brothers."

"Carl, actually. I was picking up my car." She smiled weakly. "He still works on it, always gives me a break on the cost of servicing. We broke it off but we were still friends, you know? Anyway, we heard the crash, saw the smoke go up, and went out there."

She paused, staring at her hands and the tissue they held.

"It seemed like there was nothing to be done. We parked on the shoulder. Carl told me to stay in the truck. He and Fred went over the fence. I could see the fire, it was really going, and the rest of the plane, the front part, was all torn up. Pieces were everywhere. Fred had the truck fire extinguisher. I saw him use it a couple of time, saw the white smoke stuff. I thought he was maybe saving someone."

Brenda looked up.

91

"They weren't saving anyone. I could see them, they were digging through the wreck, getting into things, like a couple of rats looking for cheese. But I didn't really understand what I was seeing, not the worst thing, not for a..." Tears filled her eyes. "They took things from people, people in the plane. Dead people."

"I see."

"It's all in the bag," she said. "Fred had found someone's laptop but tossed the bag back, because it was broken. They came back to the truck and put the jewelry bag and some stuff behind the seat. I'd stopped looking, it made me sick to think about what they were doing, you know? There were other people around and he said they better join with everyone else because it would look weird if they just took off, so they did."

"What was the other stuff they put behind the seat?"

"I don't know, it was getting dark. Maybe another bag, maybe it was all jewelry. I think there were some watches or bracelets or something. I really didn't want to look. I just wanted to get out of there."

"Then what happened?"

"They stayed until people started to leave. Then they drove me back to the garage, I got my car, and I went home. The next day, Carl came over. He wanted to put the bag, this one, into one of his hiding places. I told him no. He said this would be the last time. And he would never bother me again if I let him use it. I said all right. He used a place in the floor. Then he gave me a ring. 'For all your trouble,' he said."

Brenda looked at Deevers with a face twisted by despair and anger.

"I wanted to throw up. A ring from a dead person. He made *that* a gift."

"Which ring was it?" Deevers asked looking at the rings she had laid on the table.

"Not one of those," Brenda said. She reached into her jeans pocket and took out something wrapped in tissue. She unwrapped it slowly.

It was ornate and of a style long out of date. An emerald occupied the central setting while small, gold leaves wreathed it. Deevers picked it up and examined it. At one time, there had been lettering on the inside of the band but it was smoothed over by use and hard to make out. She put the ring down.

"Why didn't you tell him you would not let him hide it in your house?"

"Because I was afraid. Not of Carl. He has a temper, just like his brother, but he always uses words to hurt. But Fred, Fred liked to hurt people physically. And I thought if I did this one thing, they would be out of my life.

Carl was nice to me but after that night, after the crash, I realized finally he is too much like his brother to ever be anyone you'd want to be involved with, you know?"

"Why did he want to hide it at your place?"

"I don't know. He didn't say. He came in and opened a couple of the hiding places, like he was checking them for size. Then he went back to the very first one he'd opened, one in the floor, and put the bag into it. I don't know why he didn't just use it in the first place – I just wanted him done and gone." She sighed. "Back when he lived with me, he had a key. But he gave it back to me without me even asking when he moved out. Things like that, even though we weren't together, I still thought he was, underneath everything, a good guy, you know?"

"Have you talked with either brother since then?"

"No. I mean, they come into the diner, so, yes, then. But just for ordering, the weather, that kind of thing. Nothing serious."

"Did they say when they were going to come back for the jewelry?"

"No."

"And you came in now because...?"

"I heard about Fred. And I thought he got what was coming to him. Then I realized I was just as bad as him and Carl. I didn't say anything when they stole things from those dead people and I didn't do anything when Carl hid this at my house. I think I finally decided I had to do something. So here I am." She tried to smile but failed. "I guess I'm going to jail."

"We need to do a little more investigating before anything like that happens." Deevers looked at the mirror and nodded. She turned to Peterson.

"I'm going to go next door," she said. "Why don't you stay with Brenda?" Peterson nodded.

Davis met Deevers in the hall.

"He's been sitting calmly as can be," Davis said. "We haven't Mirandized Cassidy."

"Not in a hurry on her," Deevers said. "If she lawyers-up, read her her rights, but she's not the biggest fish in the pond, so I'd rather keep her on our side."

"Testimony on Carl?"

"That and helping us on whoever is after the jewelry and killed Fred."

"You think it is the jewelry?"

"Tell you the truth, I thought it would be something bigger, more valuable. Our informant was really excited about it." She shook her head. "A couple of pieces look valuable but the rest just looks like the Johnstons grabbed it in a hurry."

"Those watches? I thought one looked like a big Casio."

"Good eye. You're right. Pretty rugged, heavy thing. But the real jewelry, the necklaces, the things with gems and gold, I'm having a little trouble with the idea that some organized crime types were moving it around."

"People can go crazy over a little gold. Or maybe your CI got the whole deal wrong." Davis paused. "I really want to take down Carl. Stealing from the dead, that's pretty damned foul."

"She's our witness. Let me talk to Blasingame."

"Go for it." He went back into the observation room.

Deevers sat down in front of Blasingame and said nothing for a moment, pretending she was examining the recording controls on the wall. When she turned to look at Blasingame, she saw he was looking at her with a totally neutral gaze. No tension, no anxiety.

He was not afraid and he was not excited. Even the innocent could be worried that something would go wrong. Not Blasingame. Whatever would take place, whatever he had to deal with, he would handle it. It was like, on his scale of life experiences, being brought into a police station for questioning in connection with a murder was… Nothing. Deevers wondered at what kinds of experiences got you to that point.

"Mr. Blasingame," she said, "this conversation is being recorded. You remember that you were advised of your rights when Officer Stutz met you at Willow Run?"

"Yes, I do. I waive my right to have an attorney present at this time."

"My first question is, can you tell me your whereabouts at around 4 PM yesterday?"

"I think so. Let me get out my phone." He paused and pulled a smart phone from his pocket. He tapped on the screen, frowning slightly as he worked his way through the menus.

The most emotion he's shown since smiling at Ellen.

"Here you go." He slid the phone carefully to Deevers. "Those are my appointments for yesterday afternoon, beginning at 1 PM and until around 5:30."

"And after that?" Deevers asked as she studied the list. Shops were listed, along with their phone numbers. She copied them onto her notepad.

"I had dinner with Ellen Parker," he said. "She's the woman you saw me greet and ask to meet me for dinner tonight."

"I see." She tore the page from her notepad and handed it to Stutz. "Could you check on these for me?"

The officer nodded and stepped out of the room.

"You've been talking to a large number of people about last month's plane crash."

"I have."

"Why is that?"

"I was impressed by the way the town responded to the crash. Untrained volunteers, they tried to save who they could. You have to respect something like that."

"You were interested in particular with the people who arrived first."

"Yes."

"Why?"

"Well, they were the first of the volunteers, so there's that."

"Are you giving out humanitarian awards?"

"No. Not at all."

"According to people we talked to, you seemed to be looking for confirmation the Johnston brothers were the first on the scene."

"Once I was told they were the first, I did ask about them with other people. There seemed to be wide agreement among the townspeople the Johnston's were first. I guess because their garage was closest."

"Mr. Blasingame, Fred Johnston has been murdered."

"At 4 PM yesterday." He nodded. "Now I understand. And I've expressed an interest in him and his brother. All right." Blasingame leaned back in his chair. "I'm not here on vacation. Well, not totally."

"It would be helpful if you could be clear, Mr. Blasingame."

"I'm here looking for something. I thought I was getting close."

"Mr. Blasingame?"

"My aunt was on that plane," he said. Something flashed in his eyes, so quick that Deevers wasn't sure she saw it, something like what she'd see when looking deep into a wild cave and something in the back, in the shadows, looked back, looked at *her*, and then was gone.

"Her married name was Margaret Montgomery. She was my aunt. Her husband died eight years ago. Charles Montgomery, retired Philadelphia police."

"Why was she flying to Harrisburg?"

"Her husband's family had a gathering. They are all very close. One of the kids, I think the son of her husband's brother, was getting married. Margaret doesn't drive any more. Eye problem. She had to fly."

"Of course."

"Her daughter, she lives in Philly, her name is Mary. She can confirm everything I'm telling you. Her number is...," he reached over and took back his phone. "Here it is." Deevers copied the number, nodded, and he slid the phone back.

"You said you were looking for something."

"Aunt Margaret liked jewelry but just appearances – wasn't someone who looked for a price tag first. A lot of her stuff wasn't really expensive but she liked the pieces. To her eye, they were pretty."

"I see."

"But she had a ring, gift from her husband. It was in his family since before they came over from England in 1904. I don't know how long they had it before then. Heirloom. She wore it everywhere. And it probably was worth something. Well, then the plane crash. Do you know how the NTSB works with people's luggage and personal effects?"

"Yes."

"Yes, of course; FBI. Anyway, when my aunt's remains were returned, no ring. Likewise, the preliminary list of identified luggage did not show her jewelry bag. Mary thought, what with the fire, maybe everything had been destroyed. But the NTSB was very sure the fire had not gotten into the cargo and passenger areas. They're pretty thorough about these things, testing all of the luggage, examining it, all of that. They still have not released the luggage to the next of kin."

"It can take weeks, sometimes months."

"Right. The more information Mary got, the more concerned she became, since there was no reference to the bag or her jewelry on the NTSB list. Well, I had a chance to take some time off, so I contacted her, told her I would come on down and do some looking around."

"You said a ring. What kind?"

"Very old style emerald ring. There's like gold leaves that twist around the emerald. Over the years, I've seen it a number of times but Mary has a picture her mother took of it for insurance." He tapped his phone again and handed it back to Deevers. "That's it."

Deevers studied the image. It was the ring Brenda Cassidy said Carl Johnston gave her the day after the crash.

"Did you think you were going to find it?"

"Not really. Something like a piece of jewelry, it could have gone flying off and it's up in a tree someplace. On the other hand, I read of the responders from the town and thought there was a chance someone might have picked it up. Of course, I didn't talk about any of that with Mary."

"You were already suspicious, you thought it might have been stolen? Why?"

"I mentioned she had a small jewelry bag. Letter 'M' on it. Nothing too valuable in it but, while they found her roller bag, it wasn't there. Mary described what she thought was in it to the NTSB. They did tell her the top of her mother's roller bag was open. That was the thing that had me suspicious. Impact, sure, spring things open, but her bag had been unzipped."

"What did you think happen to it?"

"Before I came down, I was just suspicious, like I said. But when I asked questions and learned a little about the Johnstons, now I think it was stolen. I think the Johnston brothers went to the crash and looted whatever they could find they thought was valuable. I think they took her ring off her finger and dumped it off to some pawnshop somewhere."

The thing in the back of the cave looked at Deevers again.

"Mr. Blasingame, did you kill Fred Johnston?"

"No. I never met him, never talked to him. If he did steal my aunt's ring and jewelry, then I'll probably never learn the truth." He shook his head. "Killing him would have been a stupid move on my part. Hard to ask questions of a dead man."

Deevers said nothing about how Fred Johnston died – someone had asked, she thought, Fred some very hard questions.

"Why didn't you just go to the police and report the missing things?"

"Mary did. The investigators took her statement and a copy of the picture of the ring I showed you." He shrugged. "We never heard anything back."

A soft tap at the door drew Deevers into the hall after a quick nod to Blasingame. It was Stutz.

"What do you have?"

"His appointments all check out," he said. "It would have been impossible for him to snatch Fred and take him to the barn and do what was done."

"Wonderful," Deevers said. She took a few steps and looked in the other room as Chief Davis came into the hall. The jewelry was still on the table. Brenda, looking a little more composed, glanced at her but, before she could say anything, Deevers closed the door.

"Let's get an identification of the jewelry," she said to Davis.

"Take Cassidy out front," he said to Stutz, who nodded.

"What's up?" Peterson said as Stutz went into Brenda's room.

"We sort of have a motive," Deevers said. Stutz came out with Brenda and the two walked up the hall. Deevers waited until they were gone.

"Blasingame was looking for his aunt's jewelry. Her name was Montgomery. She was on the flight and stuff is missing. He says her daughter filed a report with the police."

"Which police? I haven't seen anything."

"Probably us," she said and sighed. "I need to make a call."

"And the jewelry he describes matches what Brenda brought in?"

"About to see." Deevers went back to Blasingame's room and leaned in.

"Mr. Blasingame," she said, "can you come with me?"

Blasingame rose and followed her into the hall. Deevers stopped him.

"We have some jewelry," she said. "I would like to see if you can identify any of it for us."

Blasingame nodded silently and followed her into the room. Deevers stood to one side as he walked up to the table.

"That's her bag," he said. "Her initial. I don't recognize those watches. These bracelets, I think these are hers, but I don't know about these others. This necklace, I'm almost certain that is hers. These earrings are hers, and these are as well. I don't know about these other things. They could be. She was pretty eclectic. But this ring…" He picked up the emerald ring. "Beyond all shadow of a doubt." He looked at Deevers.

"You need to have Mary take a look at these things to be sure. But the ring is hers."

"You are absolutely certain?"

"Inside the band, if you get the light right, you can see the name of the first woman who owned it." He handed the ring to Deevers. "It's mostly faded, smoothed over, but if you look at what you can see with the name 'Victoria' in mind, you can see that it fits."

Deevers tried to see it but the fluorescents were too diffuse. She reached into a coat pocket and brought out a small LED flashlight. She clicked it and maneuvered it around the ring. She clicked it off and put it away. Carefully, she put the ring on the table.

"I see it," she said.

"Would it be all right if I told Mary?"

"Yes," Deevers said. "It may be evidence and I don't know when it will be released."

"I know," he said. He half turned away and tapped the face of the phone. He put it up to his head.

"Mary? It's Bobby. Yes." He paused and took a breath. "Mary, I found it. We have your mother's ring."

Standing to one side, Deevers heard a woman cry, her voice small and distant through the phone, but clear.

After Blasingame left, Deevers called the Philadelphia FBI office. It took only a few minutes for the report from Mary Montgomery about her mother's missing jewelry to be found. While the agent on the phone tried to explain why the report had not been sent to the local police nor the task force, the only indication of Deever's anger was her abrupt termination of the call.

Her next call was to the task force. One of the agents opened a file from the National Transportation Safety Board in response to her request for information.

Right, the checked bag of Margaret Montgomery was unzipped.

"Check the notes. How full was it?"

A little hard to judge from the notes, but the photo they took during examination is pretty clear. It was pretty full. There's a note that the only thing known to be missing is a jewelry bag. I have a description of it.

"Go ahead." Deevers shook her head as she heard the jewelry bag described. "All right, thanks. Give the NTSB liaison a call and let her know we've recovered the jewelry bag and its contents. We've notified the NOK, Mary Montgomery."

Nice work. Was it...?

"Probably not," Deevers said. "Probably not."

She walked down to the Chief's office and apologized for the report's absence. He shrugged it off – bureaucracies were bureaucracies – and turned the subject to Brenda. Both of them agreed that the case against Carl Johnston would require Brenda's testimony and, whether or not any prosecutor wanted to move against her, there was nothing to be gained by holding her.

"I thought it was about the jewelry," Davis said. "But that doesn't really make sense. Some of that stuff is just one step above costume jewelry. Other than that ring, there's not much there of real value."

"I agree." Deevers frowned. "I'm going to go back over the report we received. I think I have the damned thing memorized but maybe there's something I missed."

"If there was something on that plane, say a pile of cash, it might have burned up." He frowned. "I don't think they'd try to move drugs through security at an airport, not in carry-on luggage."

"I suppose some flight crew might try it for enough money. In any case, NTSB said there was no cargo, just what the passengers checked or carried on."

"Maybe I'm wrong. Maybe there was a suitcase full of heroin." Davis' grimace suggested how little faith he had in the idea. He picked up a sheet of paper from his desk. "I guess this came in while we were talking to Blasingame." He reached across his desk and Deevers took it.

"Wonderful," she said as she read. "They confirm Blasingame's aunt was married to a Philadelphia Police Department lieutenant. He died several years ago." She shook her head and handed the paper back. "I think I've had us all on the proverbial wild goose hunt."

Before Davis could reply, Sergeant Peterson knocked on the open door.

"Come on in," he said. He saw Peterson carried a piece of paper in one hand. "What's up?"

"We got a small nibble on Blasingame."

"After all that? What is it?" Davis held out his hand and Peterson gave him the paper. Davis quickly read it and then handed it to Deevers. "You can read this," he said. "I think it's from your people." He smiled slightly.

Deevers read the page and her eyebrows went up.

"What the hell?" she asked no one.

Ellen maneuvered into a diagonal parking slot in front of Alfredo's and then sat in her car, her hands in her lap, and did nothing except wonder what she was doing.

Blasingame had left Willow Run with a police escort and she still wanted to have dinner with him.

Dinner and what else?

No answers came but after several minutes she stepped out of the car. It was a little more than half past six but the sky was still bright, the sun hidden in the west by buildings and the tops of trees. She shook her head slightly, smiled at herself, and walked into the restaurant.

A young woman stood behind a counter and smiled at her.

"Ellen Parker?" she asked and Ellen nodded. "This way."

Ellen followed her to a booth. She saw Blasingame as she approached. He slid out of the bench and stood.

"I thought I was going to have to bring a file," Ellen said.

"Only if it was in a cake," Blasingame said and smiled. "I love cake. Still, I could be on the lam. Do people use the word 'lam' anymore?""

"Then I better pay," she said as she slid into the booth. "You'll need cash for the getaway." The young woman, still smiling but with eyes getting wider, watched for a moment and then handed her a menu.

"The veal is our special tonight," she said and then left.

A waitress came and asked about drinks; both chose iced tea.

"Seriously," Ellen asked, "is everything all right?"

"For me, yes." He paused as he read the menu. "I should ask. Are you working?"

"Am I working?"

"As a reporter." He looked up. "I looked you up and read some of your articles. So, are you working?"

"I'm on vacation," she said. She felt a small wave of irritation but pushed it away; she had run into other peoples' concern with her working for a newspaper.

"It doesn't make a difference," he said, his eyes back on the menu. "There's been a murder. Of a man I wanted to talk to."

"Oh?" Ellen thought of a half dozen questions she had a sudden impulse to ask but sipped her tea instead.

"My aunt was on the plane. Some of her jewelry is missing. At least, it was. Anyway, one reason I came down here was to see if I could learn anything. I found out a couple of brothers were first on the scene and one of them is dead. They stole the jewelry and some other things."

"I understand why they wanted to talk to you."

"It was a short conversation. I have a solid alibi and a woman who was with them came forward with the stolen things." He paused and then looked up. "I talked to a friend of yours. Special Agent Karen Deevers; she was in that article you wrote about Doctor John. She seemed like a friend in the article, anyway."

"She is."

"I wasn't sure why she was involved but then I figured that, if someone was stealing things from a plane crash, there might be a federal law or something involved, so it made sense."

Ellen said nothing about the conversation she had with Karen earlier in the day but nodded.

"I'm sorry about your aunt."

"Thank you. She was one of the good ones. Actually, I knew her daughter better. She was the one I talked with. I figured, since I wanted to take a week off, maybe I could learn something. But it was the waitress from the diner that broke everything open, I think."

"Brenda?"

"She's who I saw down the hall, so I'm assuming it was her. I may be going a step too far with that."

"It sounds like it's been a long day."

"Feels long. What looks good to you?"

"Still wrestling in my mind. Have you settled on anything?"

"I'm being pulled by the lasagna, the spinach version."

"I like the tortellini with mushrooms, though this far from Philly I'm wondering if they really can do Italian here."

"We'll sue if they can't."

The waitress took their orders and for a moment a silence hung over their table. Then Blasingame asked Ellen about her hikes through the forest and that opened the door to a conversation about photography. Caught up in their conversation, they barely noticed the arrival of their food, though its fragrance stirred appetites in both and their talking down shifted as they ate.

The tortellini was good, Ellen allowed, for someplace "this far from Philly." Blasingame thought the lasagna was very good. They settled into after dinner coffee.

"How did you get good," he asked, "at moving through the forest? It sounds like you got pretty close to the deer you told me about. Are you a hunter?"

"Oh, no. When I was a girl, I spent summers on my grandfather's farm. He used to take me on long walks into the trees. He was something of a birder."

"Not a hunter?"

Ellen paused.

"No, not really, not of game. Grandpa Tom, he'd been in the Army during the Korean War and still went to the local gun club range. Some of the other men, they said he was pretty good with a rifle."

"Was he?"

"You have to know Ohio. The men back then, the older ones…" Her voice trailed off.

"Given to understatement? They're like that out in the New York farm country."

"Like that," she nodded. "They would say he was 'pretty good' and everyone would smile and you figured he could split the hairs on a gnat at a hundred yards on a windy day. Ohio."

"Good, then."

"He taught me to shoot but, when we went looking for birds, it was always with a camera." She smiled.

"When you talked about their saying he was pretty good, your accent came in. 'Oh-hi-a,' like that."

"Sorry."

"Don't be. I like accents, especially Ohio and south. You got an accent that isn't mainstream and you don't hide it, usually there's some pride that goes along with it. Too many people sound too much alike nowadays. No pride of place. In New York, everyone sounds like they come from the north Atlantic, halfway to Britain. Compared to that featureless sound, I even like Brooklyn."

Ellen laughed.

"Well, Grandpa Tom, he had the southern Ohio twang, no question. I would sound like him all summer long, while I was on his farm. Then I'd go home and try not to sound, as my father put it, 'like a hillbilly.'"

"Fathers can get things wrong."

"Including yours?"

"Of course. Like most boys, I thought he knew everything. Then I believed he got everything wrong when I was in my teens. It took me a while to separate out the stuff he really did get wrong from the things that simply wouldn't work for me."

"Like what?"

"I'm still working on that." Blasingame looked at her for a moment and then nodded. "He was an alcoholic. It killed him, eventually. He knew it would but wouldn't stop. It took me a while to realize that he didn't love me enough to keep himself alive. Not my fault, not his. He didn't have much room in him for love and the alcohol filled a lot of it in."

"Sounds pretty sad."

"There was more to him than the end. He taught me other things about loyalty, working hard, finding something that you really want to do with your life. You said your grandfather took you camera-hunting."

Ellen recognized Blasingame was diverting the discussion but went with it.

"He didn't have a very modern rig, even for back then. No telephoto, which meant he had to get close. He taught me how to step and look around. I think I sounded a bit like an elephant most of the time."

"He sounds like a country boy, someone who pays attention to the world around him."

"He did. He died a few years ago."

"Sorry to hear that. He sounds like a good man."

"Thank you. He was."

"I read your articles on-line. Do you mind if I ask you about them?"

"No, not really." Ellen held her breath, waiting to be taken back to events marked with violence and death, and waited for the questions that would reveal more about the questioner than her.

Some people approached those events with a strange kind of fascination, almost if they were titillated by the stories. Then there were the people who seemed to need the chance to assure themselves they would have done something else, something that would have brought about better results, rather than what Ellen had done. And there was a handful of people who needed to know about the nightmares, the flashbacks, as if seeking confirmation that she was damaged, now and forever.

Ellen took a breath and waited for Blasingame to reveal himself.

Though Blasingame had several questions, none were about either Doctor John or, before that, Bobby Hamme. Nothing about the rape or killing or running through the darkness or gambling her life to save two women and a child.

"About the music business you wrote about…" he started, and then asked questions that showed he had read her articles on the resurgent music scene in Philadelphia and, it appeared, was genuinely interested in it.

Finally, he nodded, obviously thinking about what she had said.

"Up in Albany," he said, "the whole music thing is weak. We don't have good venues, at least not as many, and the national artists are pretty much overlooked. There's some support for local artists but you don't see a range of music. Good jazz or blues are hard to come by, for example. The rock folks seem to be the most numerous."

"I think it's that way everywhere. But, you've got a couple of acoustical groups up there that have toured the east coast and played in Philadelphia."

"You did your research. We might. I don't follow them much. I'm more of a blues fan. So why is Philadelphia so much stronger?"

"More venues, I think. Lots of clubs, so lots of music. And not just in Philly. Small towns, thirty or forty miles away, like Kennett Square, have venues; theirs is called 'The Flash.'"

They talked more and Ellen enjoyed the feeling of being at ease. Blasingame was, she decided in those moments, "a nice guy." Not necessarily a bed partner, though she had not ruled out the possibility, but the kind of man who was reliable, straight forward. A good neighbor. A little like her grandfather, she decided, a thought that made her smile.

But there was the diversion, as if Blasingame wanted to keep her away from something, maybe something in his past. It seemed odd, given what he had volunteered. She took that as, if not a warning sign, then at least one urging caution, and wondered at her reaction. It seemed a little strong towards someone maybe not wanting to talk about a, well, *sad* part of their childhood.

They took their separate cars back to Willow Run. They found Steve, his feet up, half empty wine glass in hand, while Thomas was in the corner studying his lap top, his own glass of wine dangerously close to the machine.

"Welcome home," Steve said, waving absently. "Did you two have a good day?"

"Interesting," Ellen said.

"Pretty much," Blasingame agreed as he poured a glass of wine. He held up an empty glass and raised an eyebrow inquisitively to Ellen but she shook her head. He sat down on the couch beside her. "No kids tonight?"

"I think they've moved on," Steve said. "New couple arrived just a little while ago. I think they're in town getting something to eat."

"They are," Thomas said, his eyes on his screen.

"He cannot ignore his email," Steve said with a loud whisper. "Addiction."

"Come on," Thomas said, though his eyes did not move. "This is the first time I've checked in the past four…"

"Three."

"Three days. It doesn't make me a bad person." He smiled and looked at the small group. "I'll bet you guys have been checking your messages."

"Guilty," Blasingame said. He pulled his phone from a shirt pocket. "But, in my defense, I'd like to point out I'm actually working. Sort of."

"Not me," Ellen said. "I've been email free ever since my arrival. In fact, I haven't even answered my phone. I've tried to keep it off but I admit I've glanced at who's sent me messages. But I haven't read any." She paused. "At least, none from work."

"Addiction is a terrible thing and denial only makes it worse," Steve said.

"It's getting pretty low and I didn't bring my charger, so I'm going to have to cold turkey it."

"That's what they all say."

"Ignore him," Thomas said. "When we're home, he updates his Facebook page every ten minutes."

"Fifteen."

"The world, Stevie, is not interested in what kind of taco you are having for lunch."

"Of course, it is."

"Speaking of which," Blasingame said, looking at his phone. "I'll be on the porch."

"You see?" Steve said. "Addiction."

Blasingame grinned in reply and walked outside. He returned after a few minutes and raised his eyebrows when he saw Thomas still at his laptop. Steve laughed.

Later, when Ellen and Blasingame left the big house for their cabins, she thought the man might invite her into his but he did not. He smiled and wished her a good night and then he was gone. And that was all that happened.

Two hours after Ellen and Blasingame parted, Radisson and Bornstein saw Carl Johnston's car turn into his driveway.

A half hour earlier, they had watched a Coalville PD SUV stop in front of the house. The driver and another officer had knocked, gotten no response, and then circled the house. Apparently satisfied that no one was home, the two officers went back to their vehicle and talked to someone by radio. A decision was made and the dark vehicle pulled away from the curb, passing the two killers.

Then Carl returned home.

Bornstein and Radisson moved quickly and in a coordinated fashion – they had done this before and briefly discussed how they might handle things in this particular situation.

They drove their car behind Carl's, a maneuver that caused him to pause, his keys in his hands as he tried to recognize the two figures getting out and approaching him in the night.

"Fred sent us," Radisson said as they walked up to him. The simple sentence had the desired effect. Confused, Carl stood still as he wondered at the statement.

"Not a sound," Radisson commanded, his voice low, as he and Bornstein pushed him against his car. A gun in his face was visible even in the dark and before Carl could think of a good response, Bornstein had pushed Carl's arms behind him and ratcheted the same handcuffs used on his brother onto his wrists. A strip of duct tape went across his mouth. Radisson took the keys; they were not in a hurry to search the house with the undoubted police interest in evidence but if Carl said the case was there, they would come back. Sometimes you had to do what you had to do.

They walked Carl quickly to their SUV and put him in the same position that Fred had been in the day before, an historical coincidence that no one remarked on.

For Karen Deevers, like Carl Johnston, the day was not done, though hers ended on a much more positive note. Chief Davis, who had just ordered Sergeant Peterson to return and drop off Officer Stutz, was busy on his office telephone making calls to some of his officers to get coverage at the station and Carl Johnston's house before ordering Peterson and Stutz to go get some sleep.

Deevers called a private number and waited as it rang.

Hello. The voice was noncommittal.

"Jack, it's Karen Deevers. I got your message. Can you talk?"

Hey, sure, yes, I can. How's everything in the City of Brotherly Love?

"Don't ask, don't tell." She paused as Jack laughed; the older FBI agent had an easy sense of humor. "What do you have for me?"

Nothing critical. There will be some paperwork headed to your office tomorrow. You want a summary?

"Sure."

All right. Robert L. Blasingame is pretty clean. Is that brief enough?

"Just a tad bit more, Jack, if you can manage it."

For you, anything. Annie says to say 'Hi!' She's going up with the kids. What do we have? The guy is local, born and bred. I know you saw that notation in the CI follow-up that this bad guy Fredericks knows him but that's not too big a deal. They have met.

"What were the circumstances?"

Fredericks has a son, kid named Donald. He's attending Columbia, pre-law, so you know he's no good.

"Jack, you're a lawyer, too."

Clearly, I know what I'm talking about. No, actually, the kid is clean, at least so far. He came home to Albany for Thanksgiving three years ago. He and two buddies from high school walked into this upscale diner. Retro place, jukebox of '60's music, artisan milk shakes, whatever the hell those are, like that. Next time you and JJ get up here, I'll take you there and we'll make JJ pay for dinner.

"Deal."

So, the three kids walk into the diner. Problem for them is his dad, Fredericks Senior, is having a major problem with a guy who cornered a big piece of the drug market and Fredericks' been pushing pretty hard. The guy decides to push back in true, Hollywood-inspired, drug kingpin fashion.

"He took out the boy?"

He tried like hell. Your boy Blasingame happens to be walking up to the front of the diner, check in hand, apparently intent on going home. The two shooters are sitting at the counter and turn to do the dirty to young Donnie. Blasingame, who's standing right next to them with check and credit card in hand, grabs the gun hand of the closest one. Naturally, the idiot fires, not giving a damn that the gun is not pointed at Donnie and his companions but at the other shooter. Bullet hits the guy in his jaw and he's out of it.

"No shit."

None at all. Blasingame takes advantage of bad guy number one's understandable shock at the facial reconstruction bill he's just pulled down and twists the hand holding the gun until a whole bunch of bones in the wrist and hands break into itsy-bitsy pieces. He then holds the gun on the two wannabe perps until the boys and girls in blue arrive.

"Sounds like he was a little pumped."

My turn to say it: no shit. Okay, so Fredericks goes after the drug kingpin – I love that title, by the way – but that's not the part of the story you're interested in. Apparently, Donnie goes back to father dearest and describes Blasingame's heroism in glowing terms, like how he walked on water and only sank to his ankles.

"Doesn't sound like he had to do much exaggerating."

No, I doubt that he had to. Timing did have a lot to do with it. See, Blasingame was sitting at a table to one side of the counter. He had a view of the parking lot in front and on the side as well as anyone coming in and taking a seat at the counter, though I doubt he knew what he was seeing if he noticed the arrival of the baddies or Donnie. Anyway, timing, he was at the register at exactly the right second. I walked the scene with the local detectives; Donnie owes his guardian angel big-time for setting up that one.

"You said Donnie talked with his father?"

Yep. The old man took time out from doing a Carthage on the kingpin's butt to meet Blasingame. Fredericks didn't just shake his hand. He owns several restaurants, nice places. He was about to remodel two of them and gave Blasingame the contracts.

"Well, that's what he does, I gather."

Yep, he has a big rep in the historical restoration business up here. But that wasn't all. Fredericks' got some fingers in a dealership or three.

"Money laundering?"

One of his many paths to greatness. Anyway, he set it up so Blasingame gets all his vehicles from his dealers. He's got an F-150 up here, parked in front of his office and a Toyota Land Cruiser, white. You may see it around town down there. That thing could haul your average Abrams tank and has an MSRP north of 80K. He got a new one for pennies on the dollar a couple of years ago.

"Fredericks is big on the whole, 'thanks for saving my son' thing."

Didn't cost him anything. Remember, he's in charge of everything up here. And when he quieted down the kingpin – I still like that title – he probably got enough money from that little takeover in an afternoon to take care of the Affordable Care Act and a dozen Land Cruisers.

"He got to the kingpin? Damn, now you got me saying it."

I have a corrupting influence, something I take pride in. Let us just say, someone got to Mister Peter Domingo and three of his closest friends. I say 'someone' because we don't know who. In the old days, Fredericks might have done it himself. He was, once upon a time, a very dangerous man. And maybe he did it but his alibi seems very, very solid. No, it was someone else. Locals think he has several people who might have been up to it but we think there's no one on the local radar who has the skill set to take down Domingo and three others. We think he brought in some professional.

"'Professional?' Just one?"

The guy was spooky clean but, yeah, just one guy unless you think they managed to manipulate the video security around Domingo's home. The picture is terrible. White guy, slightly above average height, but his face was down, so we got nothing. We think he knew where the camera was. I can send you the report and copies of the stills from the video, no problem.

"When you get a chance, no hurry."

Domingo going down didn't end it. Domingo had a southern connection and, so the story goes, Fredericks had the connections followed south and scorched the earth in a pretty horrific way. I don't know if that was done by the hitter who got Domingo, it may have been a small team, but I included a summary of all that. It makes for very interesting reading, if you have a taste for the macabre.

"Anything else on Blasingame?"

Excellent reputation as a contractor and a restorer. Expensive, I am told, but very above board in all his dealings. Does a lot of pro bono work, helps Habitat for Humanity, like that.

"But no criminal history?"

Nothing as an adult. When he was a kid, they got him for joy riding. It was a buddy's parents' car, graduation celebration stupidity, and it went nowhere. He did community service and paid for a scrape in the paint.

"Military?"

None. After high school, he made his way through the state university system off and on, taking time to work, it looks like. Business major. I guess that comes in handy.

"We got one dead down here and we're looking for his brother."

I saw. You think the Johnstons found the mystery case and someone is trying to make them give it back?

110

"Yes, something like that. I thought we'd found whatever it was when we recovered a bag of jewelry from the site."

Yeah, that wasn't it. I went back over that report from the CI. He repeatedly refers to a 'case,' not a bag.

"That's the other reason I called. Has anyone gotten anything else from the CI?"

Negative. He's gone low-profile for a while. We still think something was going to Fredericks in Albany by way of Harrisburg.

"We still have eyes on his pick-up girl in Harrisburg?"

Yes, as of this afternoon. She's still in residence at that Motel 6 close to the airport. According to the staff, the first time she was there until the crash, then left. Then, as you know, she returned about a week ago. She's one of Fredericks' people, no question.

"She's still waiting. Fred is dead but she's still waiting."

Either he didn't or couldn't give it to them or they are still looking.

"I wonder why she's there. If Fredericks sent down some people to retrieve the case, I'd think they would return to New York with it."

Maybe the recovery team isn't from New York. Maybe your local kingpin, Books, I think, maybe he's doing it as a courtesy. Maybe whoever did the nasty deed isn't going back to New York when the job is done, so they needed to put the courier back in place.

"Maybe. Well, thanks for the update. Yes, send on whatever you have on the Domingo killing. You saw the email on Fred?"

Pretty brutal.

"I think, I'm not totally sure why, whoever did it is down here, looking for the case."

I get the same thought, so we're both into hunches. Mine is based on thinking all this is a prestige issue for Fredericks, so he would send his A-team. Read the report, the case may be some kind of tribute to Fredericks. Anyway, you want to keep your eyes open down there. This guy, the one who got Domingo, we think this was not a one-time thing, that he's been in business a while and knows what he's doing.

"I've encountered pros. One of them shot me. I prefer amateurs."

Hey, lady, serious for a moment. Pros don't usually mess with cops but this guy, he can be very determined. What happened to Fred also shows determination. So, eyes open wide, all right?

"No question, Jack. You know me. Very serious. Hey, tell Annie I'm thinking of her. Hug the kids for me. And take care of yourself."

Will do. Hug JJ for me and the two of you, get your butts up here before the kids finish high school.

"We will. 'Bye."

Deevers put away her phone and turned to see Chief Davis leaning against the doorframe.

"Overheard the last part," he said. "Fred Johnston might have been taken out by someone from New York?"

"They had a real pro hit a rival of Fredericks a couple of years ago. The Albany detectives think it was one of Fredericks' soldiers but the FBI office thinks it was someone from out of town."

"He may be down here?"

"Looking for that damned case, maybe," she said. "But no one's sure."

"We need to talk to Carl Johnston."

"I'm guessing we're not the only ones with that particular need."

Day Five

Chapter 5

Radisson looked down at the body of Carl Johnston and slowly shook his head. Bornstein was doing chest compressions on Carl but having no success. Radisson glanced towards the east. The morning sun was just edging into the horizon, backlighting a long line of trees in the distance. They would have to leave soon; the wooded lot they were in offered shelter from anyone on the road, but the first farmer coming across the field would see them.

Johnston still did not respond.

They had brought the young man to the wooded lot and followed a grassy road that looked to have not been used all year. Then they had started asking questions. As with his brother, Carl had encountered a twisted plastic bag but he seemed surprisingly stronger. Or so it seemed.

The man really had not wanted to say anything. Radisson thought about that. No one fought that hard for power or money. Only love…

He reached out and tapped Bornstein's shoulder.

"Hang it up," he said.

"Damn it," Bornstein said, still on his knees. "It never occurred to me he had a bad heart or whatever."

"It happens. Maybe he didn't know." He grimaced. "Long session."

"Stubborn fucker."

"I was just thinking about that. His denial of knowing where the case was seemed perfunctory."

"If you mean he stopped referring to it after the first round, you're right." He stood and brushed off his knees. "From then on it was all, 'I'm not telling you anything.' What do you make of it?"

"That he knew where the case is."

"Yeah, that's what I thought."

"I didn't know you knew CPR."

"Took the Red Cross course back in May."

"No mouth-to-mouth?"

"That's been dropped. The lungs get enough air in during the heart compressions."

"Interesting. Alright, the case is somewhere."

"Not just somewhere."

"Right – he would have given it to us except…"

"Someone has it. He was trying to protect *them*, not the case."

"That's what I'm thinking."

"What do we do now?"

"We figure out who he would want to protect."

"I think we ought to go to his house, see if there are any pictures on the mantle. If he has a mantle."

"Love of his life, huh?"

"And maybe on his Facebook page."

"Getting a little light around here. Let's go."

"Him?"

"Leave him. Doesn't make a difference if anyone finds him."

"All right."

They walked back to their car, Bornstein pausing to swipe at his knees one more time, and then they were gone.

Ellen felt confused, a sensation she did not like. She turned at the end of the driveway and saw Blasingame coming and the confusion became greater.

There was something about the man she found attractive and, at the same time, there was something about him that was distant. More correctly, something he held back, kept distant from her.

The holding back was the kind of thing that, in the past, would have shut down her interest in a man. Still, she felt herself drawn to him. That was the confusing part.

It was like something inside of her was overriding her brain and Ellen did not like the idea. She survived because she used her thinking – literally, it kept her alive.

Ellen stretched as she watched Blasingame run. He was not terribly graceful. He was almost mechanical, one leg lifting and placing a foot in front of him and the next. But he looked like he could do it all day.

"Good morning," she said as he jogged up to her.

"And to you," he said as he came to a halt. He put his hands on his hips. "I took the path into the trees, the one you mentioned. You didn't tell me it was all up hill."

Ellen smiled.

"Couldn't handle it?"

"I'm a little tuckered out," he said, breathing deeply. "Thought I was going to die, is all."

"A little sprint back to the house?"

"How good are you at CPR?"

"Oh, come on." She grinned. "Shall I give you a head start?"

Then she saw it, a flash in his eyes, and that fast it was gone.

"Say when," he said.

"Go!" she shouted and launched herself down the road.

Blasingame passed her easily, running on his toes, all the mechanical effort gone, replaced by the practiced elegant but almost violent power of a professional sprinter.

What the hell?

He was on the steps, hands on his hips, when she arrived.

"You've been holding back," Ellen gasped as she came to a stop. She heard the touch of anger in her voice and regretted it.

"No," he said. He took a deep breath. "I'm lousy at distance running. Always have been. But wind sprints, that I'm good at. High school football, coach was a believer in them. Twenty, forty yards, even a hundred, I'm pretty quick. But any further, I am a mess. 'Mister Robot,' they called me. I think too much when I'm running any kind of distance; gets in the way. Sprints, don't get a chance to think."

"You've got great form," she said. He raised an eyebrow. "Really. I did a little running in high school and college and you have great movement." She smiled. "What I saw from the fading distance."

Blasingame laughed.

"I'll want that in writing at some point," he said. "I run with a group through Washington Park most mornings. A couple of those people, they've got college cross-country backgrounds. I usually end up bleeding from my ears when one of them leads the run."

"I know the type. I try to avoid them. I hate being humiliated."

"Going to breakfast?"

"I may be able to handle a tall stack today."

"Impressive." He walked with her around the main building. "I'll see you in a bit," he said as he turned to his cabin.

"'Kay," she said, and then quickly added, "I wasn't kidding about your form."

"Thanks," he said and smiled.

In her cabin, Ellen pulled her t-shirt off and heard her phone buzz. She picked it up and grimaced. It was about out of power and, without its charger, that line of communication was going to disappear. Well, the people at work could always send her an email if it finally died. Besides, she was supposed to be on vacation.

She looked at the number and then answered.

"And what can I do for the long arm of the law?"

Morning, young lady. Did I wake you?

"No. I'm feeling both virtuous and exhausted. Did my morning run."

Ah. I'll try not to hold you up from the shower, then.

"The people at breakfast will probably thank you. What's up?"

Lunch was interrupted and I left you with the bill. Want to try again?

"Sure, if you can get free."

Hard to tell at this point. Give me a call on your way in and let's see if I can weasel my way free.

"Sounds good. I'm going to hit a bookstore and see one of the antique stores someone told me about."

Your friend Blasingame?

"Actually, no. The guy who sold me my desk." Ellen felt a little irritation but it faded quickly. "I don't know if we're friends or what."

Understood. Sorry for the assumption.

"No problem, not if you're paying for lunch."

I am. See you later.

Ellen stood for a moment, staring at her phone without really seeing it and the almost empty battery icon, before putting it down and walking into the small bathroom.

The hot shower felt good and she let the sensation fill her mind.

Blasingame was at Steve and Thomas' table, looking at Steve's tablet, when Ellen arrived.

"Good morning," she said, pausing for coffee.

"Hey," Steve said. "Omelets with five pounds of bacon."

"A little exaggeration," Thomas said. "Four at the most."

Joyce looked in from the kitchen, smiling.

"Not that bad at all, girl. What do you want?"

"A bacon omelet? Sure, but go easy on the bacon."

"A mini one for the crack reporter," Joyce said. "We have waffles. Any excuse for maple syrup."

"I'll try one and some fruit."

"Fruit cup with strawberries and kiwi. You got it." She disappeared.

Ellen sat down with the three men.

"What's up?" she asked.

"Steve's got some good pictures," Blasingame said, handing her the tablet. "He's been all over Coalville, more than me."

"I like the Nineteenth Century architecture," Steve said. "All the gothic gingerbread. Those old iron and coal barons got into contests about who could build themselves the biggest homes. You can see the same thing all over Pennsylvania."

"Steve has a book out on the subject," Thomas said. "It's been very well reviewed."

"Really?" Ellen asked as she swiped for the next picture. "These are pretty good."

"These are all done with my iPad," Steve said, his smile a little embarrassed. "It's not a bad system for taking pictures but it lacks some of the tricks of my Nikon."

"You really captured the grandeur. They look like palaces."

"More like icebergs," Steve said. His smile disappeared. "Grandeur, but very isolated. These people cut themselves off from the rest of the world and formed one of their own. Private. Peasants not allowed."

"And that's his first book," Thomas said. "The Johnstown Flood."

"Twenty million tons of water. Hard to imagine."

"You said 'peasants,'" Ellen said.

"The dam on the South Fork made Lake Conemaugh and was acquired by a man named Henry Frick. He and his buddies, people like Carnegie, turned it into a private resort. People downstream in Johnstown weren't invited, only friends of Carnegie steel." He shrugged. "They built a road on the dam, just for convenience, but they lowered the dam to do it. The spillways got clogged and then, in 1889, the rain came. The dam gave way and the wall of water, three, maybe four, stories high swept through several small places, a barbed wire factory, and into Johnstown with all the rocks and trees and other debris it had picked up at forty miles per hour. Over two thousand people died. Some burned in the debris field."

"He's always this cheerful until he's had breakfast," Thomas said.

"Sorry," Steve said.

"What happened after the flood? How did the recovery go?"

"Clara Barton came and stayed for five months. First disaster relief effort of the Red Cross. Donations came from all over the country, even from overseas. Germany, England, a bunch of countries sent money for rebuilding. Frick donated thousands and Carnegie eventually built a library."

"Frick and Carnegie? I imagine they were sued."

"Court said it was an 'Act of God,'" Steve said. "They weren't held responsible." He took a breath. "The valley Johnstown is in is prone to flooding. Mountains, snow and rain, the rivers were narrowed by dumping earth from the hills to make more flat land to build things on. But, no, the town didn't get any justice from the courts."

"The courts," Blasingame said quietly, "are about the law. Sometimes, justice has to be found elsewhere."

No one said anything for a moment and Joyce came with the first platters of food.

"I knew some of the story," Ellen said. "How did your book do?"

"Well, it's paid for itself," Steve said, slightly waving a piece of waffle on the end of his fork. "And it gave me the idea for the book on the houses of the barons. Which is called, if you want to hit a book store, 'Houses of the Pennsylvania Barons.'"

"The pictures," Thomas said, "are more dramatic than the title."

"And the flood book?"

"'Johnstown: Track of the Flood.' I used photos from the flood and contrasted them with how the same places look today. It's co-authored with John Worth, a geologist. He showed me how the flood hit Johnstown twice."

"Twice? How did it do that?"

"Have to buy the book," Steve said, grinning. "Seriously, no, you don't have to. I'll give you copies of both, autographed." He looked at Blasingame, who was consulting his phone. "For both of you," he added.

"Already bought them," Blasingame said, holding up his phone. "I'll send them to you for the autographs."

"And I don't take books for free," Ellen said. "Not from writers. Tough enough getting published and I'd feel like I was stealing from you."

"That's sweet. Tell you what. I go nowhere without a box of author's copies."

"He does," Thomas said, wiping his mouth. "One-man PR agency."

119

"Hush. You're giving away my plan to rule the world." Steve turned back to Ellen. "Let me give you the books and you donate the costs to the American Red Cross." He grinned. "I still like Ms. Barton."

"Deal. I like her, too." Ellen cocked her head to one side. "So, twice?"

"The first wave went through the town but couldn't all go through when the downstream course became clogged from all the debris. But with all the water still coming, it backed up into the feeder creeks. Then everything that backed up came back down." Steve shook his head. "The town got hammered twice and from more than one direction."

The conversation drifted away from Johnstown, gently aided by Ellen. Pennsylvania could be as dark as the coal in its hills, she thought, and there were places where no one had walked in a century and the sun's light never touched the ground. She experienced some of that darkness, had nearly died in Pennsylvania's hills. With help and the firm anchor of friends who met and overcome their own darkness, she healed. But she learned something about herself, something about darkness.

Thus it was Ellen Parker sat at a table and shared breakfast with three people, smiling, talking, laughing, and hid her secret: some of the darkness ran through her and always had.

Perhaps everyone had a touch of darkness, but it seemed to Ellen, most tried to pretend they did not. She understood the pretense. It was the biggest hurdle in her healing. Maybe some of it was genetic; she remembered Grandpa Tom, a man who, for all his gentle love with her, was a dangerous man on the hills of Korea and southern Ohio. Or maybe it was a natural part of being human, something making people capable of being killers, something that could put a person on a wire, and wires could break.

And, sometimes, the person could break the wire deliberately. Then there was darkness without end.

After breakfast, Blasingame went to talk to an antique dealer and Steve and Thomas, still teasing one another, drove off to do whatever it was they were going to do. Ellen took her two new books back to her cabin and put them beside her cell phone.

She thumbed it on – the low battery icon reminded her of her failure to pack the charger – and checked for text messages but there were none. Gratefully she turned the phone off. Well, she was on vacation and had promised herself no calls, no text, no email. Ellen smiled; it was a great promise, but hard to live with. For a reporter, cutting the electronic communications cord was a little like going through withdrawal.

Even as she thought that, she turned on her laptop and looked at the list of her email. *All right, I see the messages but I am not going to read them.* She shut the lid and, for a second, felt virtuous. Then she grabbed her car keys and almost fled from her cabin, smiling all the way to her car.

I've escaped!

Chief Davis, Sergeant Peterson beside him, looked up from some papers as Karen Deevers walked into the police station.

"What's the good word, agent?"

"Not much, chief," Deevers said, shaking her head slightly. "Do you have anything?"

"We're running checks on out of state plates and giving New Yorkers a priority. No one is holding their breath – we get tourists and antique dealers from Maryland, New Jersey, and New York, so there's a lot to run through the computer." He shook his head, mimicking Deever's motion. "Of course, there's nothing that says they couldn't have borrowed a car with Pennsylvania plates."

"A very long shot."

"Yes, ma'am, but it would be nice if there was a match with one of those interesting fellows on your most wanted list."

"It might simplify all our lives."

"Do you think they are still around, still looking?"

"The pick-up person is still sitting in her motel north of Harrisburg," Deevers said. "To me, that suggests several possibilities. If the bad guy or guys had the thing, then I think she's waiting for them to drop it off. We might spot them do it. On the other hand, if they determined it could not be retrieved, she would be gone, just like when the plane crashed." She smiled grimly. "When she came back, the alarm bells really went off and everyone blessed the agent who wouldn't let anyone question her when she left – we don't think she ever spotted our people. She's still *there* so, unless they are burning down the turnpike to deliver it as I speak, they are still *here* and they are still working on getting it back."

"Whatever it is." Davis took a breath and let it out slowly. "Still no idea what the hell it is?"

"No, sir. Something carried onto the aircraft, not checked. Our CI still hasn't surfaced, so we haven't been able to ask any more questions."

"Almost have to be cash, don't you think?"

Deevers paused long enough Davis' eyebrows climbed up his forehead while Peterson's eyes narrowed and she knew both men were wondering if they were about to get some "FBI bullshit." Local law enforcement always was suspicious of the Feds and she had worked hard to be as open as she could be.

"We don't think," she said slowly, "our CI would know about or be involved in the movement of money. That's not his area of expertise. But he's involved. What he handles are high value items – jewelry, paintings, art things, gems, those kinds of things. Someone wants to carry some heavy wealth, he's the guy who converts their cash into diamonds, *the* international currency, good anywhere. That's as close to moving cash as he comes. He's done some smuggling and has connections to overseas buyers as well as domestic."

The eyebrows came down a little.

"Interesting. But why would he know about it at all? Your briefing said the thing was going to that guy up in New York state, what's his name?"

"Fredericks," Peterson said. "Runs Albany and has a finger in some other pies."

"Right, Fredericks. So how does a fence get involved? You made it sound more like the thing was a gift to Fredericks. Is he already planning on selling it to the highest bidder or what?"

"A good question," Deevers said. "The truth is, we don't know, not for certain. A couple of our people think this is some kind of payment, maybe a peace offering." She shrugged.

"Peace offering? You mentioned the payment thing before but this is the first I heard about a 'peace offering.'" The eyebrows began their climb back up the chief's forehead and Deevers felt Davis' steady cop-gaze on her like a hot light.

"It's a guess," she said. "We're clutching at straws, trying to figure this whole thing out." She took a breath. "With the break-down of the traditional organized crime structure, a lot of locals slowly moved into the chaos of the crime and drug business and gradually gained some semblance of control."

"Fredericks in Albany, Books down here in Chester County, got it."

"Exactly. Same pattern up and down the east coast, west through Cleveland to Chicago, and so on. Nature abhors a vacuum, so you get people moving in to impose order and, of course, a lot of the cowboys have matured. They have their turf, enemies are pushed out, now they need stability for their logistics. New era, new organizations, alliances, working partnerships, structure. Thing is, the old structure also supplied a system for resolution of conflicts."

"Besides blowing people away."

"Right. There's no council, no body of people to take disagreements to, not like the old days. There's a tendency on our part to miss some of the consolidation in the ongoing noise from the street-level druggies fighting for street corners, but we're becoming aware of it. It is happening."

"All right, consolidation. Maybe it brings a system for some kind of arbitration, a way of settling disputes. If that is happening, how does the thing fit in as a gift?"

"It's guesswork but here's the reasoning." Deevers stopped as Peterson held up a finger and walked over to the always-on coffee urn and poured cups. He brought them back to her and the chief.

"I figure this is going to take a while," he said and smiled as he took a sip.

Deevers nodded her thanks and took a sip. It was terrible but it was coffee and promised the existence of civilization.

"I have to warn you," she said. "This is hard-core guesswork. We haven't even bounced this off the rest of the task force, mostly out of concern of losing what little credibility we 'fee-bees' have here in the Keystone State."

"It's not that bad," Davis said. "If the FBI said the sky was blue, I'd only look twice to confirm it." He smiled and Deevers returned it.

She lost the smile and frowned slightly. "You remember me telling you about the drug guy who sent the guys who tried to kill Fredericks' boy?"

"Stumbled into our Mr. Blasingame, you said."

"Which led us to waste time putting eyes on Blasingame." She shrugged. "Thing was, the druggie, name of Domingo, was in a pipeline coming up from south of here. We know it wasn't Baltimore but someone south of that, maybe DC, maybe, but more likely Virginia. They ran Domingo, used him to gain a toehold in New York state. Apparently, Fredericks decided to follow the pipeline and kill whoever was at the other end."

"He really took it personally."

"And then some. The agents in Albany heard last year a small team from New York went down asking questions in the fashion used on Fred Johnston."

She paused to take a sip. "The story goes on that the team nearly got to the end of the pipeline before whoever it was in charge down there apologized profusely and offered up one of his own in penance, the guy who had directly worked with the late Mr. Domingo."

"That would be rough on organizational morale."

"As would being dead. At the point of the apology, Fredericks' people had killed half a dozen and had the guy in charge down there firmly in their sights. Rats were rowing madly away from the ship. Business was neglected. Fredericks wasn't interested in taking over, this was personal, an affront to his prestige. When he got the word offering the deal, he took it." Another sip. "Domingo's handler was turned over to Frederick's hitters."

"Shit," Peterson said softly.

"How did he know it really was the guy working with Domingo?" Davis grimaced. "Never mind. They did a 'Q and A' like they did with Fred."

"Now, all that, up to that point, is fairly solid, only a little guesswork. The rest is speculation. The case on the airplane, our people think, is a gift, just a way of making sure it all is settled. It's like tribute to Caesar, something Fredericks would appreciate. Not cash, not drugs. Personal." She shook her head. "There's no organized crime council, no body of people to serve as arbitrators. Fredericks' mad dogs were called off because of the plea of his target. Man to man. Primitive. Not sophisticated, not yet. So, yes, someone is paying tribute to Caesar. And Caesar called off his legion."

"What do you get for the criminal who has everything?"

"And that's the interesting part. Fredericks doesn't just collect piles of money. He's an art lover. Big time. In this scenario, the case is holding some art thing."

"I see where your CI would fit in, then. You said he knows about art things. Maybe he helped pick the gift out."

"Maybe." Deevers shook her head. "Speculation. On the other hand, maybe it's a bunch of negotiable bearer bonds, maybe it's a bunch of diamonds. Maybe it's a drug buy and we've gotten romantic about the issue."

"Maybe it's the head of Alfredo Garcia. All right, that makes things maybe a little more real. Weird, but real." He turned to Peterson. "We have eyes on Carl Johnston's house."

"We're trying to maintain around the clock," Peterson said. "It's slowing down the plate checks, but that can't be helped." He shook his head. "If we're going to break this open, we've got to find him before the bad guys."

"Brenda's due here in about ten to talk with you, as per your request," Davis said, glancing at his wristwatch.

"Small gamble letting her go home yesterday." Deevers smiled slightly. "I appreciate the cooperation."

"Arrest her and she might have lawyered up," Davis said, frowning slightly. "I think your move to keep her on our side was the right one." He smiled. "In addition to everything else we were doing overnight, we went by her house several times. Had to have our patrol go lights out and nose into her drive to check her – she's to hell and gone off the main road. She hasn't budged."

"Glad to hear that."

"Since Carl didn't come home last night, I think you might want to explore that with her."

"I agree. Who will be in the booth?"

"I've got it," Davis said. "Sarge will be out checking plates."

"Good," Deevers said, nodding. "Anything you hear that we need to discuss, please interrupt."

"All right. I don't know, given the winding down of their relationship, how much information Carl might share with her, but, hell, we're due for a break." The chief paused to take finish off the last of his coffee. He smiled. "Sooner or later he has to turn up."

Todd Stoltzfus, most of his work for the morning done, walked towards the large wooded lot bordering the narrow road and studied it as he approached. Extending the farm into it was an idea his father toyed with periodically but, with the rise in corn prices, now took more seriously.

Todd favored expanding the farm's tilled land but was not sure the wooded lot was the place to do it. Its low-lying position collected water and the roadside drainage ditch bordering the lot would likely need clearing. Naturally, his father gave him the task of gathering the information needed for a decision.

Todd smiled as he walked. Since Todd's graduation from high school, his father increased his emphasis on his son's involvement in decisions about the farm. Todd enjoyed being called on for tasks like evaluating the lot. As far back as he could remember, taking on responsibility around the farm was a part of his life and he loved it.

He had the higher than average maturity Mennonite children usually had but he was, after all, eighteen, and so he was thinking about something else, someone else he thought he might love, as he stepped over the sagging barbed wire fence bordering the lot. He carefully disengaged a barb catching a boot lace. As he straightened, his thoughts almost immediately went to the image of a young girl's face and his smile returned.

For several seconds, the young girl's face seemed to compete with what he saw, almost like it was trying to protect him, but then reality's image pushed everything else away.

A body lay twenty feet away, next to a dirt track coming into the lot from the road. Surrounded by weeds and brush, blue jean clad knees and the dull red of a work shirt contrasted with the green and brown.

Todd did not panic, did not turn around and run the half mile back to his house. Though part of his mind already guessed what he would find, he knew he could not be certain and whoever lay in the lot might need his help. Even as he formed his thoughts, he moved towards the body.

It was a man, older than Todd. His half-open eyes stared up at the sky and saw nothing of its bright blue. Todd crouched beside him and willed his hand forward to search for a pulse. The man's arms were under him, hiding his wrists, so Todd felt the man's neck.

It was a thing he would never forget, a thing cold with some of the last moisture of the night collected on it, leaving the cold flesh damp. Todd pressed, searching, but there was nothing. He stood, still feeling the neck on the tips of his fingers, and turned his head, looking towards his home.

Now he would run.

Brenda did not appear to have gained much sleep overnight; her eyes were heavy with fatigue. Still, she seemed alert and focused on Deevers, who nodded to herself.

Past the trauma of making a decision and now was settling in. Let's see if she's going to back-track on what she's said.

"How are you doing, Brenda?"

"Pretty well." The younger woman paused. "I feel like I got some weight off my shoulders."

"Good. I'm glad to hear that. Some of what you told us has already helped."

"Really?"

"Really." Deevers smiled. "It turns out that ring you returned belonged to a crash victim and her daughter was afraid it was lost forever. It was a family heirloom. It was really important to her."

"That's... I can understand that. I'm glad I brought it back." She looked down at her hands and then back up at Deevers as she wiped her eyes. "Listen, I know I was in possession of stolen goods. I'm guilty of that. I thought about it all night. I haven't been told about my rights, so I guess I'm not under arrest yet." Brenda held up her hand from the table as Deevers started to speak. "Let me get this out while I still have the nerve," she said, smiling slightly.

"I want to go to nursing school, but if I have a felony conviction, I'll never get licensed as a nurse. I know that. But here it is. I've got to see this through, nursing school or whatever. I don't want a lawyer or any of that. Ask me anything you want, search my house, my car, my bank account, whatever you need. I just want to get it done. I just want..." Brenda stopped, her eyes flooded. She pulled a tissue from her purse almost angrily and wiped her eyes.

"Damn it," she said. "I promised myself I wasn't going to do this." She put the tissue away and looked at Deevers. "I just want to do the right thing."

Deevers said nothing for a moment, studying the woman's face. It was a mixture of fear and determination.

"All right," Deevers said. "Where do you think Carl went? Maybe someone he knows that he worked for, maybe buddies in the drug business."

"Not to Mr. Books," Brenda said. "You know him, right? The guy who everyone thinks runs things around here?" Deevers nodded.

"Fred worked for Books," Brenda explained. "Time to time, but Carl just followed Fred. Fred did all the deals. Carl was just... You know, like day labor for Fred. Carl is afraid of Books, like a lot of people in the drug business. Carl thinks Books has people killed who cause him trouble. Maybe he's seen too many movies, I don't know, but he wouldn't go to Books if he was in trouble."

"I see. Well, where else might he go? We really want to find him before anything bad happens."

"His parents passed on years ago. I would say he would come to me, even though we're officially broken up, but..." She grimaced. "I imagine he's heard by now that I turned the jewelry in, so I guess he'll avoid me like the plague. He doesn't have any other relatives he's ever mentioned. The guys he hung around with in school, and there weren't many, have pretty much moved on. He never talks about them."

"What about friends of Fred's?"

Brenda laughed.

"They were all druggies. God only knows what happened to them. His biggest buddy OD'd two years ago. I think the only other guy he hung out with at all found Jesus, went to rehab, and moved away. People, places, things, all that. Fred's last girlfriend, I think she would shoot on sight either of the brothers. Her name was Crystal Smith. That was her name, it wasn't about the drugs she used. She's in Philly, the last I heard."

"Does Carl have a girlfriend, maybe someone before he met you, or someone he took up with after you dropped him?"

"Thanks for not saying someone he has on the side. He might have, I don't know, but I kind of doubt it. He isn't a real good liar, not like Fred. I think I would have known. Before me, just girls in high school, mostly ones looking for drugs. You know." Brenda took a long breath. "See, I was really stupid and ignorant. I didn't know about a lot of this stuff, what he was into. Other people did, people who knew him in school, but I didn't know him then. Different crowd. When I started unhooking myself from him, then people kind of filled me in."

"Does he have a cabin, another residence somewhere?"

"Fred did," Brenda said, nodding. "Kind of a fishing shack south of here. But they accidentally burned it down a couple of years ago trying to mix some speed. The police found some of their equipment. It wasn't really Fred's, he just used it. All Fred has is his house."

"Camper, RV, anything like that?"

"Unless they are working on one at the garage, no. But the garage, I just remembered, sometimes when they are working real late, you know, rush job, they would stay overnight. They have these old Army cots you can unfold and beat-up sleeping bags. I don't think either of them used them in the past year but that stuff should all be there."

"Is there anything else you can tell us about Carl's whereabouts?"

"Not really. Well, he might doze off in the truck. Not the tow truck. Carl's. They both used it but it belonged to Carl. He usually left it at the garage and would go home in his car but it's a full-size pick-up with a crew cab. You could curl up in back."

"Thanks, Brenda."

"Look," Brenda said, "for how screwed up Carl became, he isn't like his brother. He never had a gun that I saw. People say he is a good mechanic and I know he is a good carpenter from all the work he did on my house. He's done a lot of carpentry for people all over town and everyone says he's pretty good at it, you know? He put the steps in at the back of the diner. He helped Fred, but Fred could be pretty mean. Violent, you know? Carl isn't like that. I still think that if his brother wasn't around, he would have been a good guy." She took a breath. "I'm not excusing him, just trying to explain. He's not dangerous." She smiled slightly. "He couldn't really be, you know? What with his heart and all."

"His heart?"

"He has a condition, it kept him out of the PA Guard. He has to watch his stress, the doctor told him. He mostly got himself off of drugs because of it." She paused. "Maybe because of me, too. I don't know about that. But he's not a violent guy. When you catch him, you know, try to remember that."

"We will," Deevers said. "Really."

"Thanks."

Knuckles rapped twice on the door before it opened. Sergeant Peterson, his face so still it might have been carved from dark wood, leaned in, glanced at Brenda, and then looked at Deevers.

"A moment, agent," he said.

Radisson and Bornstein saw the police car, a dark SUV, as they drove towards Carl's house. It had been a lousy night, what with Carl up and dying before they were ready for him to do that, and finding a police car outside of Carl's house seemed to be just fucking perfect.

"Keep going," Bornstein said unnecessarily.

"Got it."

"This really sucks. And I… Is he leaving? Damn, he's fired up his lights."

"I am a good citizen," Radisson said, "and I will let the officer pull out in front of me. Always be courteous to police officers."

"Good advice. Hold off parking until he's out of sight."

"Already on top of that. He does seem in a hurry."

"You don't suppose someone found young Carl?"

"Could be. All right, I'm parking. See anyone?"

"No one in any windows. Maybe everyone's at work."

"Maybe." He shut off the engine. "All right, can you reach the jacket?"

"Yes, and I have the clipboard." Bornstein pulled the red windbreaker with the reflective lime stripes from the backseat.

"Don't forget the hat."

"Oops." He reached back again and then put a red baseball cap on. "I am a master of disguise," he said as he slipped on sunglasses.

"Quick in and out."

"Just your friendly neighborhood power inspector, looking for a problem," Bornstein said as he climbed out of the car. He closed the door and then paused as if reading something on the clipboard. He looked around slowly and then walked back towards Carl's house.

Radisson watched him turn into the driveway and stop at the front door. No one came in response to his use of the doorbell and then, when that failed, his knock. Bornstein looked around and then tried the door. It was locked.

Bornstein studied his clipboard as he walked toward the side of the house and then turned the corner. Radisson grimaced; this was the part he didn't like, not being able to see where the other man was and what was happening to him. Pennsylvania, probably every other house had someone with a gun in it, some lunatic who would start shooting at the drop of a hat. He shook his head. Too many crazy people around nowadays. It made everything more difficult.

As the minutes passed, his partner did not immediately re-appear and Radisson took that as good news. He repeatedly looked around but saw no one.

Wait, there was someone. In the rearview mirror, he saw a middle-aged woman, small, thin, wearing shorts and a red sweatshirt with a white T on it, snaky white lines leading to iPod ear pieces slightly hidden under bouncing gray hair. The woman was on the sidewalk and looked like she could run all day.

She was abreast of Carl's house and Radisson watched her closely, waiting to see if she looked in the direction of the house. She didn't and he started to let go of the breath he had held. Then he saw Bornstein step around the corner of the house and freeze.

She kept running and did not seem to notice the figure in the red windbreaker. Bornstein didn't move, didn't want to attract her attention. Radisson pulled his cell phone free and put it against his ear, blocking her view of his face as she jogged past.

A moment later, Bornstein slid into the passenger seat, shaking his head.

"We are due for a break."

"She didn't even pause," Radisson said as he carefully pulled out into the street. "She's still going, like that damned battery bunny."

"'Bye, bunny," Bornstein said as the woman turned the corner.

"And...?"

"And, if we were detectives, we would say we just found a couple of clues." He took off the jacket and cap, stuffing them behind Radisson's seat. He held up the clipboard. "Take a look at this."

Radisson glanced at the clipboard and saw a crude floor plan sketched onto a long, yellow page from a legal pad.

"What is it?"

"Floor plan of some place but the part that caught my eye was I think he noted where there are little hiding places."

"Say again?"

"Keep your eyes on the road. He had a bunch of these sketches. Most had addresses on them, people's names, with little notes, like, 'bookcase' or 'replacement stairs.' Rough drawings, like what you would do before getting really specific. Thing that caught my eye was, for each of the things he had a tiny, dashed-line image, like he was planning where it would go in the house."

"What, he was some kind of carpenter? I thought he was a mechanic."

"Modern era, old man. Everyone has to have more than one career. That kind of economy. I blame Obama. Anyway, yeah, I found a leather bag of carpentry tools beside the front door and there are a bunch of power tools down in his basement. A stack of these marked 'Done' with a date. He's been doing this stuff for a couple of years."

"And the one you took?"

"Not in the stack. It was in his desk, right hand drawer. Like he wanted to refer to it. He has these little rectangles in the floor and some views of where they would be in the wall. In the corner, there's a sketch of how to open one in the floor. Some kind of lever action with a floorboard. At least, that's what it looks like."

"Man, are you thinking this is some kind of treasure map?"

"Study it when we get back to the motel, see what you think. But, yeah, I think these are hiding places in someone's house – the floor plan doesn't match his."

"He and his brother helped move product."

"It makes sense they might need some place away from the garage to hide shit. Maybe they used it for the case."

"Logical, but I don't suppose he was kind enough to put the address on the drawing?"

"No."

"Bastard. I'm glad he died. Why are you grinning?"

"I said 'clues,' plural." Radisson saw him take the yellow page off the clipboard, revealing a color photograph.

"Love of his life? Be still my beating heart. Where did you find it?"

"Bulletin board beside the desk his laptop sits on. I moved a take-out menu over so the empty space isn't obvious."

"Good move."

"I think you are right about her being his girlfriend. He really had a mantle, fireplace and everything. You're going to love this. Guess who was in the only framed picture on it?"

"This girl?"

"Yep. I thought someone might notice a missing picture from there and was delighted to find this one, so I left the other."

"She looks familiar."

"Keep your eyes on the road. That's what I thought."

"From…?"

"Can't remember." Bornstein shook his head. "Too tired to think straight. We've been up all night. Someone in town here? You have any ideas?"

Radisson shook his head and stifled a yawn.

"We're keeping terrible hours," he said and Bornstein chuckled. "Let's get back to the motel and get a nap in. She's familiar but it might be wishful thinking."

"Maybe a clerk or someone we saw in town."

"Maybe. You want to get something to eat?"

"Sleep first, eat second."

"Sounds like a plan. Hit that diner later?"

"Sure, why not?" Radisson yawned. "Old fashioned diners usually have good food."

Ellen found Blasingame on the front porch of the big cabin. He had various pieces of hardware spread out. He studied them each carefully and looked up as she walked through the door.

"Hey," she said. "Going over your loot?"

"Hey, back. Got a call from a client and I'm trying to see if any of the things I already found will work for her."

"She needs hinges?" Ellen nodded at the rows of metal.

"And latches, suitable for fairly heavy shutters." He shook his head. "She was going to remodel without them but changed her mind. Now she wants to do period shutters and use matching hardware." He gestured at a set. "She needs those but enough for seven more windows and I think that means I have to go back into town. I think the guy I got these from has more, fingers crossed." He started to put the other hardware into a pair of plastic crates and Ellen knelt down to help.

"Thanks."

"Glad to help."

"Are you going into town?"

"I've got it in my head I need a set of book shelves."

"How big?"

"I'm thinking a two or three row about as wide as the desk I bought."

"That would be 54 inches wide, 36 inches deep."

"You remembered?"

"Mind like a steel trap. Actually, I talked to Kelly after you bought it. He was pretty happy you got it. You don't have room for a set of shelves off the desk?"

"I might, but it would be for stuff I want close by, so it would have to be narrow to fit. My office room is a small, second bedroom."

"Kelly has several different sets of book shelves," Blasingame said as he brushed his hands against one another. "I think he has a couple that might work." He picked up one of the crates and Ellen took the other.

She followed him back to his cabin and they put them down on the floor.

"Are you going in now?"

"I was going to try…"

Her cell buzzed, surprising Ellen – she thought she had turned it off to preserve its fading battery – and she fished it out of her jeans, glancing at the screen.

"Oops, my boss," she said. "Sorry, have to take this." Blasingame grinned as she walked out of his cabin

Hey, Ellen. Having a good vacation?

That was her boss. No 'Hello,' no self-identification. Bang, and into it.

"Enjoying myself, Sam," Ellen said and smiled at the truth of it.

Got a stringer coming over for the Johnston thing, probably with an intern in tow. You stay on vacation. You need it. All right if they call you? The intern thinks you walk on water.

"Flattery will get you everything. But my cell is just about dead and I don't have a charger. Tell them to email me and I can call them or do a face-to-face." She paused. "There may be something going on."

Yeah, we picked up a lead from a trooper. Deep background at present. All right, keep an eye on your email. I'll call the stringer, Daryl Jennings. You know him.

"I do. Covers Coatesville."

And Coalville because we didn't have anyone else close. Intern is Tammy Wynette.

Sam's humor; the intern was Tami Wilson but Sam couldn't resist. She paused as Blasingame walked by. She mouthed, "Good luck" to him and he smiled again.

"Got it, Sam. And thanks for letting me loose."

Stop it – there will be violins next. 'Bye.

And Sam was gone. Ellen shook her head but grinned. While she felt the familiar urge to find the story, she knew she needed a break. Besides, she disliked having to spar with Karen Deevers in the traditional cop and newsie dance.

Ellen glanced at the battery symbol and raised an eyebrow. That was *low*! She decided to turn her phone off and save it for emergencies. She heard Blasingame's car driving away and thought about lunch but decided to check her email through her laptop. Maybe Jennings would contact her quickly.

Daryl Jennings' email waited for her. Jennings suggested meeting at the bed and breakfast and Ellen readily agreed. Twenty minutes later, she sat on the front porch as Jennings' faded blue Volvo came down the driveway.

Daryl Jennings was one of those men who seem to get to an age and then stop aging. Ellen had met him first several years previously. He was an older white man carrying too much weight who peered with a bit of amusement at the world through his gold-rimmed glasses. He had a habit of running his fingers through his loose blond hair. As he climbed out of his car, smiling at Ellen, some of the weight was gone but everything else was still there, including the gold-rimmed glasses and an expression suggesting the world was a series of not very good clown acts.

"Ellen," he said, extending his hand, "we simply must stop meeting like this. People might talk. Good to see you again."

"You, too, Daryl," she said, shaking his hand. "Hey, Tami," she said as the intern, a tall Oriental woman emerged from the passenger side. "Sam said you'd be coming."

"Spending the week with Daryl," she said, raising her eyebrows, as if signaling something about the assignment. "Learning all about stringers."

"I'm trying to talk her into another career entirely," Jennings said. "Sam said your cell was about shot."

"True. I left my charger at home."

"On vacation, you're entitled." He glanced at the big building. "I know of Willow Run B and B, but the key question has to be, is the coffee any good?"

"It's on me, yes, and I'll give you some background."

"Great, lead on."

There wasn't anyone else in the main room, though Ellen could hear Patti doing something in the kitchen. They went into the dining area, fixed coffee, Ellen waved at Patti, and they returned to the main room.

Ellen walked the other two through what had happened. Daryl took notes on a small pad and did not look up as she talked. Tami, her eyes a little wide, forgot to sip at her coffee as she heard the story.

"The task force," Daryl said when Ellen paused. He looked at her over her glasses. "Has it announced itself? I haven't heard or seen anything about it."

"The announcement about Fred Johnston's death came from Coalville PD. You've seen it?"

"Yes. We got our email copy on the way here."

"So they didn't do it at a conference. Passing reference to looking for his brother, Carl, but didn't describe him as missing. All of that from CPD and no federal people in sight."

"Low profile, then."

"Why is that?" Tami asked. Daryl smiled.

"They might not want anyone to know," Daryl said, "because they don't want people running away, which is what I would do if the FBI announced it had moved into the neighborhood and was interested in crimes I was responsible for." He looked at Ellen. "Have they suggested anything about leads?"

"No." She paused. "They have mostly been eliminating people who might have been involved."

"The Johnston brothers stole from the crash. Any other connection?"

"Nothing announced."

"Fred Johnston," Daryl said slowly, putting his pad away, "was a known bottom feeder. He goes back a few years, mostly running errands for the local big cheese, a man named Tallman. I've heard the new boss is a fellow by the name of Books but nothing about Books using him. Fred also stole cars and did a little dealing. Ran a couple of meth labs and, so the story goes, managed to damn near blow himself up in one five or six years ago. Largely regarded as an idiot, but a dangerous one. Poor impulse control. Maybe that's why Books hasn't used him much, if at all. His brother…" He shrugged. "Not much. A little bit of a reputation but nothing serious. A follower."

He looked at Ellen for a moment.

"Your friend, Special Agent Karen Deevers…"

"She's bounced ideas off of me, all in deep background. Speculation and suspicion. She's asked me to hold onto things for now. I'll let her know you are taking over and you two can get together."

"Ah. Got it. All right. We don't want her to think you've violated confidentiality, then, right?"

"Right. But she hasn't shared very much. You've met her?"

"No, but I know of her." He nodded. "I think this may end up being mostly handled by the locals, and I have met them. Coalville's PD has a decent rep. Chief Davis is a no nonsense, old fashioned kind of guy and his number two, Sergeant Peterson, is pretty similar. I think we'll see if we can get a conversation going with the Chief, find out what they are looking at." He shook his head. "From what I've heard about Fred, someone could have been unhappy with him for any of a number of reasons, including robbing the dead in that crash."

"Well," Ellen said, feeling a little uncomfortable, "there's a lot of focus on the plane, but you might be right about people having reasons to come after him that have nothing to do with his connection to it."

"Well, maybe. Hell of a coincidence, though." He looked at Tami. "Let's go see Chief Davis and Agent Deevers and hear what, if anything, they have to say. And you," he turned back to Ellen, "Mister Sam said to remind you to remain on vacation."

"To hear is to obey," Ellen said, smiling. "It's all yours."

Ellen watched Daryl and Tami drive away and returned Daryl's wave. She thought she would feel relieved at Daryl officially taking over the story and getting back to her vacation. But what she felt was a sense of… What was it? A little anxiety? Why?

There was a piece to what was going on she wasn't seeing. She went back into the main room and gathered up the used coffee cups and walked them to the kitchen, her mind tugging at things. Patti, sitting at a small table and reading a newspaper, looked up.

"Thanks," she said and smiled. "Just leave them. Newlyweds came in late last night and he took breakfast back to his bride. They haven't emerged, been in there all day, so I'll have a few more to do when they finally come out of their cabin."

"They liked breakfast that much?"

"Right, it was my breakfast that has them enraptured." She lay the paper down. "Do I have to give you the talk on the birds and bees?"

"Let me go get my notepad," Ellen said, leaning against the sink and folding her arms.

"All right, here's how it goes. Boy meets girl, or boy, or girl meets girl, but, anyway, one damned thing leads to another and the dishwasher ends up having to wait."

"I think you left a couple of steps out."

"That would explain my confused life. Are you going into town?"

Ellen glanced at her watch and nodded.

"I wanted to swing over to Kelly's and check on a bookshelf. Maybe see if my friend Karen is free for a late lunch."

"Don't rush – he's open to 5:30."

"All right." Ellen walked out to the porch and took out her cell phone. The low battery icon seemed to glow as she hit Deevers' speed dial number.

There was no answer and she was turned over to Karen's voice telling her to leave a message.

"It's Ellen," she said. "Daryl Jennings, our local stringer, is taking over and may be in touch with you. I've only discussed things with him on background. He's also going to try to Chief Davis, who he knows. I'm coming into town and will look to see if you're there and up for a late lunch. Have a good one."

Ellen shut the phone down, almost feeling guilty about using it when it had so little juice. Karen, she thought, was probably already at lunch.

Special Agent Karen Deevers was not thinking about lunch as she stared at the still body of Carl Johnston. Beside his head, a plastic bag similar to the one that killed his brother lay crumbled in the weeds.

137

"It wasn't the bag," she said, shaking her head and remembering Brenda's remarks about Carl's heart. Peterson nodded in agreement but remained silent.

"Agent Deevers?"

She turned towards a county deputy, who pointed back down the weed-covered track leading to the road.

"Ma'am, we found a tire track."

For a moment, while looking at Carl's body, Deevers had felt like there was only her and him, a world defined by the living and the dead, but the deputy's reference to something that might be evidence broke the wall surrounding her. There were police of various agencies all around, a paramedic team waiting on the road, and a half dozen people in civilian clothes wearing blue windbreakers like hers, though hers was the only one with *FBI* on the back. The others had various samplings of the alphabet denoting their agencies but, except for the forensic people collecting bits and pieces of things, all moved aside as she followed the deputy.

The tire print was the outside two-thirds of a tread and about six inches long, preserved in what had been a puddle and now was just a smear of mud. She crouched to examine it. A ruler lay beside it, used by a hovering photographer who, as he stepped aside, pointed at it.

"Lug," he said. Deevers nodded.

The imprint was very clean, clean enough that she could see one of the lug prints was not whole, not like the others. Something had cut it.

"Lovely," she said.

Peterson looked at the weeds and pointed as he described the movement of the killers' vehicle.

"They came in nose-first and stopped closer to where we found the body. Out of sight from the road. When they left, they backed up to here and then pulled in, going off the track, so they could go face first onto the road." He looked up and down the track as Deevers stood. "If they had stayed on the track and just backed all the way out, they wouldn't have left anything."

"They made a mistake. If we can find their vehicle, we can match the tire print." She nodded to the forensic technician, who smiled back, enjoying the FBI agent's recognition of his job.

"We're still checking New York vehicles," Peterson said. "The tire print might point us to specific makes and models, narrow the field a little." He shrugged. "If they are replacement tires, we can still look for the manufacturer and model. We've been handed a break."

"I'll let our people know," Deevers said. "If they got what they wanted from Carl, they are probably on their way to Harrisburg to drop it off."

"I don't think they did," Peterson said as she took out her phone. "I think Carl screwed them and up and died on them before they learned anything. That bag didn't kill him. So they still don't know where it is. I think."

Deevers nodded and then spoke into her phone. In a moment, she passed on her information. She paused, listening, and then nodded silently. She exchanged a few quick words and put her phone away.

"No one has showed at the motel. The woman slept in and is eating pancakes for lunch as we stand here."

"They are still in town. They don't have it."

"We still have a shot."

"I'm just wondering who they have on their list to question next."

Deevers nodded, silent for a moment as she thought.

"The Johnston brothers were back-up players to Books, the local power, right? How about this for an idea? The people who came hunting the Johnstons didn't do it by accident. Maybe they knew who the local thieves were and went right at them."

"That might work," Peterson said, watching the forensic tech mix up dental stone for taking a cast of the tire print while another carefully surrounded the imprint with low plastic gardening wall. "We thought it was Blasingame because he asked questions, but his alibi for Fred was solid. We'll check for Carl but I doubt there will be any alarm bells. No one else asked about who responded to the crash, so, yeah, maybe they already had some names in mind."

"Did the Johnstons work with any people regularly, enough that our killers might naturally expect them to be in on it?"

"Not that we're aware of. The Johnstons were bottom feeders, just used for simple crap. Fred was the most deeply involved, but, as I said, they kept him out of the big stuff because of his unreliability. Carl just followed his lead. We didn't have anything suggesting they had regular relationships with any of Books' people." Peterson paused. "But it's worth thinking about. We know a couple of people we might ask."

"Ask quietly. If Books thinks we're looking at his organization for all this, he'll probably scream to New York to pull their people out and the game will be over."

"I agree. It would be nice to think they were stymied. If they hold still long enough, we'll find their damned car."

Ellen took a late lunch at the diner and was delighted that Karen came by.

"How did you know I was here?" Ellen asked as Karen sat down.

"FBI. We know everything." She smiled. "If only. I got your message at the same time I saw your Honda on the other side of the square and gambled you were here."

They placed their orders and Karen leaned back and took a deep breath.

"Long day?"

"And it's only lunch time," Karen said. She shook her head. "Well, late lunch time."

"Hey, I want to give you a heads' up."

"Your stringer, Jennings? He already came by the police station. I heard him introduce himself to the chief. But I slipped past him."

"How'd you manage that?"

"FBI. We can be very stealthy. Have you given him what we've talked about?"

"No."

"Good girl. I appreciate that. Is he a jerk?"

"No. He has a good reputation. He knows a lot about the local crime scene. Knew about both of the Johnstons."

"Both of the ex- Johnstons, I am afraid. Rules still apply, all right?"

"All right."

"Carl is dead. Farmer found his body. Bad heart, we think, but the bad guys had him."

"Crap."

"We are exploring the possibility the Johnston's were in someone's sights before they ever got here. And the Johnstons might be involved with some of the local heavy hitters. It doesn't make much sense that they would know how to fence what they may have found. They would almost have to talk to someone bigger than they were to find out how to turn it into real cash if they didn't just dump it into some pawn shop somewhere." She paused. "Whatever the hell it is, or was."

"That makes sense."

Karen paused as their food arrived and then looked around.

"I don't see Brenda." She took a sip of iced tea. "Brave woman, coming forward with the stuff Carl dumped with her. That bastard talked her into holding onto stolen goods; could result in real legal problems for her."

"Even with Carl dead?"

"Even. She knew he had put the bag into a hiding place he built into her floor. Accessory."

"Hiding place?"

"When he lived with her, he did some work on the house. While he was at it, he built in some hiding places. Probably hid drugs and shit in them back then. Anyway, she dug out a jewelry bag he put in one and turned it and a ring he gave her into the locals. The ring, by the way, that he had to have taken off the finger of a dead woman."

"Pretty foul."

"But Brenda brought it all in. The whole thing tore her up. Might screw things up for her, but she brought them in. I'm not surprised she's not in. Probably needs a few days to get her feet under her again."

"She probably hasn't heard about Carl yet."

"That might improve her morale."

"I knew she had brought the jewelry in. Bob told me over dinner."

"Bob did, did he? And what other things did Bob whisper in your ear?" Karen grinned as she stabbed her salad with her fork. "Or are the two of you past the whispering part?"

"Well, actually…"

"Don't tell me. Willow B and B; he flies a multi-colored flag?"

"No, it's not that."

"Good. I was having a rich fantasy life about the two of you. The man's shoulders…" She shook her head and then lightly snapped her teeth together.

"I'm going to tell JJ."

"He'll love it. Have you noticed his shoulders? Never mind, don't answer. I don't want to know. But things haven't happened with Mr. Blasingame?"

"No." Ellen paused. "I think it's mostly me. He's a nice enough guy and really looks great. You should see him without his shirt. But, there's like this wall."

"A wall? Around what?"

"I don't know. I just think there's something else there with him, something he doesn't want me to see."

Karen nodded.

"You might be wrong about that," she said, "but you might be right. I think you have to trust your instincts. Nothing has to be rushed." She wiped her lips with a napkin. "He looks pretty straight arrow from a law enforcement perspective, but we haven't gotten around to building records of peoples' sexual suitability."

"Yet."

"Liberal media hack."

"Fascist enforcer of the oligarchy."

"Which reminds me…" Deevers paused, frowning slightly. "Something just occurred to me. Carl and his carpentry…" She looked at Ellen. "Listen, I have to go."

"Go, go. Hope you're right, whatever it is."

"Something staring us in the face," Deevers said as she slid to the aisle. "We've overlooked the obvious."

Then she was gone. Ellen looked around, realized she was stuck with the bill, grinned, and waved for the waitress.

"You're right about it being obvious," Chief Davis to Deevers. "We're going to need a warrant."

"Right, I'll get a statement ready. We want both brothers' houses."

"And outbuildings, and the garage."

"I'm going to make a call and get us some additional hands. I don't want to break up your people's search for New York plates."

"That's a damned thin reed, but, yeah, we ought to keep it going." He shook his head. "I think you are on to something. Given all the bullshit those two idiots were involved in over the years, it makes sense Carl would have turned their houses and garage into a honeycomb of hidden places." He nodded. "I let county know about your idea that the bad guys have a list of names, people who worked with Fred. They had no flash of light, as they don't know of anyone who has strong links to Fred – he was not the kind of guy who anyone would want to partner up with – but they are checking."

"I think we're really ahead of the bad guys on this," Deevers said as she took out her cell phone.

After paying for lunch, Ellen walked to Kelly's and they spent some time trying small bookshelves on the desk, something he was not in favor of.

They paused so he could switch on more lights; it was getting dark outside and he said something about rain moving in.

He put a set of shelves on the desk and then backed away, his hand on his chin. He said nothing, but frowned.

"I agree," Ellen said.

"It just looks awkward."

"My problem is I just don't have a lot of space for book shelves in my room."

"There's another option. How about a custom set of shelves made to fit the desk? Matched for wood, stain, all that, something would look like it belonged. That guy I was telling you about could do it in his sleep."

"Sure, but..."

"There's the cost, I know. Let me give him a call, he's already got the pictures I sent him when I asked him to think about restoring it, and let's see what he says."

"All right."

For a moment, Kelly said nothing. Then he folded his arms.

"I may have just really, really screwed up."

"You said he was near Kennett Square, restorer." Ellen looked at him, her gaze steady. "You're going to tell me your guy is Michael Klemmer."

"He is." Kelly grimaced. "I didn't know you two knew each other when we talked about the desk the first time. I'd read your series on women vets but I didn't read the other stuff, so I didn't know. But I read them this morning. I'm really sorry."

Ellen smiled slowly and Kelly fell silent.

"It's all right," she said.

"I was just afraid that I would stir up..."

"It's all right. He's a good guy."

"Yeah, he is. You saved his life."

"He does good work. But, listen, when you contact him, don't tell him it's for me."

"You don't want to take advantage of his thanks?"

"He might double his price. After all, he did get shot in the leg."

Kelly laughed, shaking his head. He looked relieved.

"All right, all right," he said. "I've got your cell and I'll call you as..."

"I'm just about out of charge. Send me an email. I've got my laptop plugged in."

"Not a problem. And I'll keep your name out of it, if you really want me to."

"I do."

"Michael, Kelly."

Hello, Kelly.

"Remember that desk I talked to you about a couple of weeks ago, the one that had its roller top taken off?"

I do. Travesty. Do you want to make a run at restoring it after all?

"No. I found a kindred spirit, someone who seems to love it as it is. Wants it because it's not from Ikea. I'm going to take some pictures of it after she starts using it and include it in that article I told you about."

Nice to hear it's going to be used.

"But she needs some bookshelves and would like to have a small set *on* it. Maybe as wide. Matched to the desk."

It would have to be matched to the desktop stain, not the sides, or it's going to look awful. Maybe a box, use the desktop for the bottom shelf and then one above it with back and sides for support, something like that?

"Yes, like that. Can you sketch out some ideas and costs?"

Sure. When do you need them?

"Well, she's here on vacation. What I'd like to do is, since we're going to deliver the desk, is have the shelf unit go along with it. It would be great if you could get some ideas to me in the next several days."

I'll do a couple of sketches tonight and get them to you in the morning. If she green-lights it, I could have it done in a few days. After that, though, I'm going to be tied up with a couple of other projects.

"Understood. Glad to hear you're busy."

You said 'kindred spirit.' She knows about antiques?

"Not really. But she likes things made by people. The touch of a human hand."

She sounds like a crafts person.

"No. Not that I know of. Well, maybe she is. I don't know."

Well, all right. I'll get something to you very late tonight or early tomorrow.

"Thank you, Mike."

Kelly put away his phone slid his hand across the top of the desk. He had fought with himself to keep from saying anything that might remind Klemmer of Ellen Parker.

That might remind Mike of an afternoon in his parking lot when he faced a killer and was saved by a young woman. He shook his head as if clearing it of a nightmare that wasn't his. *I can't imagine what it must have been laying there, a bullet in my leg, and the only thing keeping me from death was Ellen Parker. And she looks so...*

Normal.

Radisson and Bornstein slept until late afternoon. Both felt a little groggy even as they drove the short distance to the diner.

"The drawing."

"Carl's drawing?"

"Yes. It didn't match Carl's house. But what about Fred's?"

"You think they would build hidey-holes for drugs in their own homes?"

"No." Bornstein sighed, frustrated. "Of course not. It's got to be someone else."

"Don't give up hope. We agree he was trying to protect someone and you found that picture. If we were cops, that would be a lead."

"She still seems familiar to you?"

"Yes. Still can't say from where."

"Don't try to force it. That never works."

"My clock is out of whack," Radisson said as he got out of the car. "It feels like it's really late but the sun is still up." He glanced upward and shook his head as he looked at the sun and then at his watch. "A little after four is all it is."

"Know what you mean. I'm going to do a couple of laps when we get back and try to get some more sleep."

Radisson nodded. The difficulty with recovering from overnight work was a sign of old age, he thought. Back when he was a youngster, he would go home in the dawn, brush his teeth, change his clothes, and be out and about without a pause. Nowadays he preferred to go to bed with the late news and sleep a full eight hours. He sighed as he followed his lover into the diner. Probably a good idea to get out of the job. Something for younger men.

He slid into a booth and looked around as his hands picked up a menu. Something...

"I got it. That woman." Radisson's voice was barely a whisper. "I remembered just as I sat down. She works *here*. I saw her taking orders when we drove by a day or so ago."

"No shit." Bornstein's eyes were wide.

"None at all. I'm certain I saw her."

"I wonder when she gets off work."

"Maybe we can give her a ride home."

"I don't see her."

"Different shift? Has a cold?"

"Maybe she's in mourning. Be right back." Bornstein put his menu down and walked to the register, taking out his wallet as he did. A waitress appeared and he leaned towards her, speaking softly. He smiled and made a self-deprecating shrug.

The waitress smiled back and reached to a shelf under the register and emerged with an envelope. He slipped a bill into it, sealed it, and wrote something on it. He smiled again and handed it to the waitress. Then he came back to the booth, still smiling.

"Told her we stiffed a waitress here the other day. Just stupidly forgot. You know how men are."

"I believe I do."

"Stop it. Anyway, after I described her, she said, why, that's Brenda. She has called off for today, won't be in. Lady referred to an old friend dying."

"That he was and did. Did she mention Brenda's last name?"

"She didn't and I couldn't think of a reason for asking for it."

"No sense making the connection more obvious than we have to."

He paused as the waitress came to their booth. They gave their orders and sat silently for several minutes.

"Need her last name," Radisson said, looking towards the register.

Bornstein nodded.

"I have an idea," Radisson said. He slid out of the booth and walked to the register. He seemed to glance at the waitress standing beside it but did not pause. He turned into the restroom at the end of the diner. A few minutes later, just after the waitress brought large mugs of coffee, he walked back. He seemed to be in no hurry, his gaze idly looking out towards the square and then back into the diner.

He sat down and leaned back into the thick booth seat. He was smiling.

"All right, Mister Smarty," Bornstein said, "what have you learned?"

"Cassidy," Radisson said. "Time card on the wall behind the register."

"I was looking right at it and didn't see it," Bornstein said. "Good eyes. We are in business."

"Indeed, we are."

Bornstein took out his phone and then put it away as the waitress returned with their food. He and Radisson smiled at one another.

In business.

Ellen paused on the sidewalk and let the dark blue Chevy Suburban pass through the intersection. One of the two white men in front glanced at her from behind heavily tinted aviator sunglasses; though he wore a sport coat similar in style to that of the driver's, he didn't wear a tie. She wondered at the sunglasses, since the clouds were becoming denser, threatening rain, and drawing the color and light out of everything.

She crossed the street and walked to her car, eying the sky. Ellen could smell rain in the air and she smiled as she closed the door.

Safe.

Ellen drove carefully. In the late afternoon, there were people getting off from work and some seemed pushing to beat the coming rain. She circled the town square and went east on Stanford Avenue. Recognizing quickly she had gotten turned around by the square, she looked for a road heading north. Clear of the town, she found one quickly and turned left and soon picked up speed heading to Willow Run.

There was something about the road…

One damned thing after another. Patti's phrase came, though, for a heartbeat, she did not know why nor why it had something to do with the road she was driving.

No, the road I was on. Stanford. Becomes the county road. And Brenda lives on it.

One damned thing after another…

Ellen pulled over and stopped, frowning as she concentrated. Then her phone buzzed, almost shocking in its intrusion.

"I thought I turned you off," she said as she pulled it from her jeans. She punched it on.

Hey, it's Bob.

Blasingame – the sound of his voice pulled her focus away from trying to solve the puzzle.

"Hey, yourself. What's up?"

I just ran into Patti. Are you still there? You're fading.

"Yes, yes, I am. I'm just about out of juice."

Got you. She said you were in town and I'm done working. Want to meet?

"On my way back to the B and B. But I... Wait a sec."

Maybe it was because she was not trying to force it that the understanding came. *One damn thing after another – Fred, Carl, and Brenda...*

"Bob, can you still hear me?"

Yes, no problem. What's wrong? Whether or not it was happening, he sounded as if he was slipping into the distance.

"It's Brenda, Brenda from the diner."

I know her. What about her?

"She was Carl Johnston's girlfriend. He gave her things from the crash."

I know about that. She had my aunt's jewelry...

"Right, right. But Carl had hiding places in her house. Maybe she didn't know about all of them. Bob?"

For several heartbeats, there was no reply.

...You hear me?

"Yes. Did you hear what I said about the hidden things at Brenda's house?"

Right, hidden things.

"The guys looking for things may go for her next. Maybe they heard she turned in some jewelry. We've got to let the police know."

Say again.

"We've got to let the police know."

The police, right. I'll do it, I'm in town. You're hard to hear. Are you still...?

Her phone shut down, displaying a notification about needing to charge, and then the screen was black. Ellen tried to turn it back on but nothing happened.

She sat very still, her eyes clenched, her hand tight on the silent phone, commanding herself to think. Whoever killed the Johnstons might be looking for Brenda. Blasingame would tell the police and they would move to protect her.

Then she remembered Brenda was not at the diner. If she was at her home, then she needed to be warned. Ellen put her phone down on the seat next to her slowly. *That damned charger...* All right, there was only one thing to be done.

Ellen checked for traffic and then did a rapid U-turn. She sped down to the county road that Stanford Avenue had become. If she couldn't call, she would have to go out to Brenda's and tell her to come into town.

She turned at the intersection and looked for the red mailbox, remembering it from her conversation with Brenda. For a moment she saw nothing and wondered if it was possible she had passed it before turning north and never noticed. But then she saw it.

Corn grew in dark rows on either side of the county road and, while the red mailbox was in plain sight, the drive it flanked curved and disappeared behind trees and shrubs. Ellen's foot came off the gas and pressed the brake as she prepared to turn.

Then she saw in the far end of the drive, the back of a dark SUV and, beside it, the Frankencar.

Someone else was at Brenda's.

Ellen looked ahead. The corn came up almost to the asphalt, held back by a shallow drainage ditch. Slowing down, she looked for any spot that she might get the Honda onto. Finally, she pulled across the road and, facing in the wrong direction, brought her car to a stop on the shoulder. Her car, with its left wheels almost at the bottom of the shallow ditch, seemed to hang at an awkward angle.

Ellen picked up her phone and tried to turn it on. It flickered and then announced it was shutting down. She dropped it and opened the glove compartment. Her hand found things and discarded them – a plastic envelope of registration and proof of insurance forms, a box of tissues, a hammer-like device for breaking car windows made her hand pause before moving on, a folded map, another one, a small packet of tissues, a tube of Bee's lip balm, some quarters, and, finally, an old, small Gerber multi-tool. She grabbed it and stuffed it into a pocket as she got out of the car.

She glanced upward. The clouds still threatened rain and were even darker than before. She crossed the ditch and immediately was in tall corn.

It was still green and towered above her. The ground, shielded by the stalks and leaves, was mostly bare and soft. A cold breeze, maybe a forewarning of a coming storm, made the corn rattle as the stiff leaves struck one another.

The rows were contour plowed, curving around the slight rise in the ground as it spread away from the road. Ellen turned and followed the row. It curved to her right, but slowly, so she stayed with it, thinking she would be able to see Brenda's house before turning away from it.

Then the curve sharpened and more rows to her left appeared. She nodded. The farmer contour plowed and then, as he followed the contour away from the road, he had more room to put in additional rows. Where she had just had one row to her left when next to the road, now she saw six or more. She squatted, getting under most of the leaves, but saw nothing other than corn stalks.

She stepped between the rows, walking what she thought was towards the house. Ellen had taken only a few steps, not enough to see anything even when squatting, when she heard men talking. Their low voices were unclear. Were they at the cars? That seemed right. Maybe they were the police.

Maybe they are not.

Ellen looked to her right, down the curving rows. She turned in that direction and moved as quietly as she could, though she thought any sounds she made were masked by the breeze and the drumming corn.

In a moment, the rows turned again, this time to the left. Had the farmer worked around the house? She followed the row, now marching in a straight line until it was lost to the broad leaves of the stalks and dark shadows from the coming storm. Ellen heard a distant roll of thunder.

She turned to her left and stepped through the rows, bending down to look ahead. Ellen saw the grass of a yard first with a garden shed just beyond the corn. Then she saw the house.

It was a single-story white ranch. A screen door to the kitchen was slightly off-set from the center of the back wall and bright lights let her see into the house clearly.

She could see Brenda Cassidy sitting in a chair but it was a second before she saw that the young woman was bound to the chair with duct tape.

They were not the police.

Ellen did not see anyone else, nor could she hear the voices. Her lips tight, she hesitated for a heartbeat and then she sprinted out of the corn, dashing the short distance to the kitchen door's steps. She skidded to a halt, going down on one knee, and pressed herself against the wall.

As her hand jerked the multi-tool out of her pocket, she listened and thought she could hear the voices again. She took a breath and opened the door.

She stepped into the kitchen. Brenda, her eyes wide, turned her head and followed her but said nothing. Ellen pulled the small knife blade free from the folding handle of the multi-tool.

She sliced down through the tape on Brenda's wrists and blessed the Gerber people – the thing was almost scarily sharp.

Cutting Brenda free of the chair was more complicated. The tape went around the back of the chair, so she had to cut it loose at either edge.

The last slash cut through Brenda's t-shirt and met flesh. Brenda's breath hissed through her clenched teeth but she made no other sound. Blood welled even as Brenda stood. Both women stepped back to the door and Brenda pushed it open, more slowly than Ellen had opened it. Then they were outside with a rising wind. Brenda turned to one side but Ellen grabbed her elbow.

"This way," she whispered in a voice barely heard above the wind. "My car."

Brenda nodded and they hurried into the corn, backtracking Ellen's trail. As they entered the corn, the rain came suddenly and massively, spattering on the corn with an almost deafening percussion that seemed louder than the storm and its occasional thunder.

Ellen could see where she had stepped and followed her own footprints. Then she heard a man's shout. It was hard to determine its source. Was it from ahead?

They turned, paralleling the yard and following the contoured ranks of the corn field. When they came to the first curve, Ellen paused, trying to see ahead.

It was like looking into a tunnel. The corn rows pressed in from either side and the storm's rain made everything dissolve in a dark grayness that seemed to hide every evil hidden thing Ellen could imagine. Part of her wanted to stay in place, but the other part of her understood if anyone chose to pursue them, they only had to look in the corn rows to see the footprints the two women left. They had to keep moving, they had to get to Ellen's car.

Ellen walked crouched, reaching up to push the corn leaves aside, though it did little to improve visibility for there was nothing but darkness ahead. Her other hand was held by Brenda and she glanced back at her. Brenda held her side but she just nodded to Ellen.

Ellen saw the curve ahead, the one that would take them parallel to the road. As she started to turn, she felt Brenda's grip jerk away. She turned and saw a white man with close-cropped hair standing over Brenda's body.

She launched herself at the man, reaching for his eyes, but something slammed into her from the side, taking away her breath and dropping her on Brenda.

151

Ellen could not hear anything for a second but then a man's voice seemed to come through the sensation of never being able to breathe again.

"Holy shit. Someone ate her Wheaties this morning. I thought she was going to rip your ears off."

"She was quick. You have the tape?"

"Absolutely, but maybe we might want to just leave her here."

"No, let's see if she can help us with Ms. Cassidy. Object lesson, maybe."

Ellen was flipped onto her face and her hands were pinned behind her. She felt duct tape bind her wrists together. Another piece went across her mouth. She waited for a tsunami of fear to engulf her, a legacy of a dark night and the hands of a serial killer, but all she felt was an intense focus on what was happening. Her mind was looking for openings, ways out, a chance to survive. Whatever she had left behind from that night, she had taken with her a will to survive.

"You'll have a chance to talk later," one of the men said. Then she was pulled to her feet, though there was little strength in her legs and she almost fell. A hand slapped her butt.

"Hey, try harder," the man said and grabbed her arm hard enough to leave a bruise. She was walked, almost dragged, through the corn rows and then she was in the yard. She looked around her but only saw the Frankencar at the side of the house and the rear of the dark SUV beyond it before they reached the back door.

Rough hands put her in a chair and she felt the duct tape encircle her. Ellen saw an unconscious Brenda next to her. One man, the man with the close-cropped hair, held her up while the other, the one looking a little younger, quickly wound the tape around her and then her wrists.

With Brenda secured, though still slumped forward, the older man stepped over to Ellen. He reached up and took the tape away from her face as the younger one patted her pockets.

"Now, who are you?"

Ellen did not answer but the two men were not willing to wait. She felt a hand force its way into her jeans and take out her wallet.

"Ellen Parker," the younger man said. "She has a press ID."

"Really?" The older man leaned forward. "Let me see. Philadelphia Enquirer. Never heard of it."

"I have. It's real."

"All right." He straightened up. He smiled but his eyes were expressionless. "Ellen Parker of the Philadelphia Enquirer, why are you here?"

Again, Ellen remained silent, believing time was her only ally. If Blasingame had called the police immediately, how long would it take them to send someone out to Brenda's house? She glanced at Brenda and saw blood dripping from her nose.

"I'm a friend of hers," Ellen said slowly. "I just came by to visit."

"News people," the older man said, shaking his head and still smiling, "don't have friends. Again, why are you here?"

Before she could respond, the younger man reached in front of her. In his hand was her multi-tool.

"This is nice," he said. "See, a little knife blade, couple of screw drivers, opens to pliers, really neat. And fucking mad-dog sharp."

"I'll get you one for your birthday," the older man said. The younger man barked a laugh. Then he unfolded the multi-tool so the pliers were exposed.

"Want to take a couple of her teeth?" he asked calmly. "I've only got the one bag."

"And we do want to save it. All right." The older man took the pliers and opened and closed them. "It is nice." He leaned forward so his face was directly in front of Ellen's. He smiled.

"You've lost teeth," he said calmly. "Sure, you have. Everyone has. Maybe the dentist had to take one. But have you ever had one ripped out of your mouth without anesthetics? And then another?" He shook his head slowly. "I am told it is one of the most painful experiences available to people, right up there with burning." He held up the pliers and opened and closed the jaws. "The longest I've ever seen anyone hold out was three, but I always thought he was ready to go at two, it was just that everyone was pissed at his delaying, you know?"

"I came out here," she said, "doing a story on the murders of the two brothers who stole things from the dead. She used to be the girlfriend of one."

"Used to be?"

"They broke up last year. Her ex left some stolen jewelry with her and she turned it in."

"Turned it in?" The younger man asked from behind her.

"What did she turn in?" the older man asked, his face still inches from hers.

"The police haven't said," Ellen said. Her mind realized she and Brenda were close to death but the more she talked, the longer she was alive. And there was no point in lying. "There's been an investigation going on since the crash. Relatives reported things missing. The crash investigators called in the FBI. That got some attention from the paper but the deaths of the Johnston brothers got me sent out here. Trying to beat the TV people."

"She was holding what they stole," he said, nodding. "Pretty much what we thought. Unfortunately, Carl wasn't more forthcoming. Neither was his brother."

"Fred is dead," the younger man said and the older man smiled again.

"Do you think," he asked Ellen, "that we are here for a bunch of costume jewelry?" His hand whipped across her face, stunning her.

The pain throbbed into existence and across her cheek she felt a line of fire. He had used the hand holding the multi-tool. Something moved down her cheek to her throat and Ellen realized it was blood.

"You need to tell us a bit more."

She raised her head and the man behind her gripped her forehead and pinched her nose shut. The older man, still smiling, held up the pliers in front of her, squeezed them open and closed, and told her, "Here we go."

Ellen fought to keep her mouth closed but she had to curl her lips back to breathe. The older man carefully reached and pinched her upper lip, raising it. She saw the pliers come closer. She tried twisting her head away but the man behind her had her in a tight grip and it was as if she was in a vise. She kicked out, striking the older man in the leg, but he ignored any pain it caused, though his smile disappeared.

Brenda groaned and the pliers paused, held just in front of Ellen's nose. The older man looked at Brenda.

"Cinderella is waking up."

"Think that was Snow White," the younger man said as he released Ellen's head. He reached over and pulled Brenda's hair, raising her face. Her eyes slowly opened and the older man moved in front of her.

"Brenda Cassidy," he said, "good to be talking to you again. Have you recovered from your little jaunt into the corn? I regret leaving you unattended earlier, but we needed a drawing your ex-boyfriend made and we left it in our car. Silly us. Now, shall we get back to business? I hope I don't have to repeat myself – you know the question I need answered. Where, oh, where is the case? It's about this big," he drew a rectangle in the air with his hands.

"Living room," Brenda said, her voice small, as if she was a distance away from Ellen instead of being almost shoulder to shoulder. "All the big hidey places are in the living room. Has to be there…"

The younger man's hand appeared, holding a sheet of paper.

"Layout matches," he said quietly and the older man nodded as he took the paper.

"There are three cubby-holes in the living room," he said. "Which one would you say it is in, dear Brenda?"

"The jewelry was in one, the one to the left of the front door. Near the side wall."

"Got it."

"There's nothing else in it. One next to the couch is empty."

"Near the hall?"

Brenda nodded and he smiled. She took a deep breath.

"I never looked in the last one. I don't know what's in it."

"This one?" He touched the paper and she nodded.

"Closest to the front door, on the right, in the floor." She took a deep breath. "Throw rug and end table on it. Like the others; push on the side of the board next to the wall. It will come up and then you can raise the other ones, the other boards. But I don't know if there's anything there at all." It seemed to take all her strength to say it and the younger man released her hair and let her head fall forward.

"Well, that was nice and cooperative," the younger man said.

"Mmm, perhaps. Bring her. She'll open it for us." He handed the multi-tool to the younger man.

"You think maybe booby-trap?" he said as he took the tool.

"She's the one with the boobies. Let's let her find out."

The younger man snorted a half laugh. He cut Brenda's tape loose from the chair but left her hands bound for the moment. He stood her up by her hair. The older man now had a gun in his hand. He touched Brenda's nose with it.

"Now, be cooperative and don't think you can outrun a nine-millimeter bullet. Take us to it." He glanced at Ellen. "Try not to get lonely. We'll be back for you in a minute or two."

The two men walked Brenda out of the kitchen and into a hallway. Ellen heard their shoes on bare wood and then there was silence.

Ellen fought with the tight tape. Her wrists gained some space but she could not free them. It felt like she was losing skin but she kept twisting her wrists.

Ellen paused when she heard the younger man say something. The older man laughed and then spoke.

"Exactly right. Put it in the car."

"You got it."

Ellen heard a house door open and then there was a muffled explosion of sound that included Brenda's yelp of pain.

"Stupid bitch."

"You all right?"

"Yeah, yeah. You want to…" She couldn't hear the rest of what the man said. The front door closed and for several minutes there was silence, interrupted by a distant, slow roll of thunder. The rain intensified, fell off, and then increased in volume.

The older man came into the kitchen, dragging an unconscious Brenda by her arm. He released her next to Ellen's chair. Ellen heard the heavy sound of a car door closing from the front of the house.

"What is it with the women around here?" he asked. He studied his wrist, looking at the band of his watch. "I think she broke it." He holstered his pistol and undid the band. "Broken all to hell," he said, grimacing and shaking his head as he studied it. He looked down at Brenda. "Fucking bitch." He kicked her in the side without a lot of effort and returned to examining his watch. Finally, he sighed, shaking his head. Folding up his watch, he slipped it into his pocket.

"Well, I guess I'll be able to afford a new one."

He looked up at another distant peel of thunder. Then he took his gun out. He stepped to Ellen and smiled as he put the muzzle a few inches from her face.

"I think it is time for us to say goodbye."

"Easy, Daniel," Robert Blasingame said from behind him.

Ellen could not see Blasingame; the older man blocked her sight. The gun in her face did not move and her breathing stopped. For several seconds, no one said anything.

"Blasingame?" he asked.

"Yes."

"This isn't the plan. What are you doing here?"

"You know why."

"We just found it. We were about to take it to…"

"To San Diego. We know."

Again, there was silence.

"Michael?" the man asked, and Ellen thought she heard despair in his voice.

"Sorry, Daniel."

"Ah, dammit."

For the first time, the muzzle of the pistol wavered. Then it became steady again. The silence returned.

"Why am I still alive?"

"Why do you think?"

"That Mr. Fredericks wants to cut me a break does not seem a likely answer."

"No. He doesn't want *her* dead."

"Reporter. I get it. Too much heat. How about if I…"

The gunshot slammed through the room and something warm and wet sprayed across Ellen's face even as she instinctively ducked. The older man fell between her and Brenda.

Ellen slowly opened her eyes. Blasingame was crouched over the older man, feeling his neck. The sleeves of his windbreaker were covered in blood. He looked up at her.

"I'll get you a towel," he said. He went to the sink and wet the end of a hand towel. He stepped back to her and wiped her face. His expression was serious, as if the task was the most important thing he had to do. He wiped her dry and then tossed the towel to the sink.

"Sorry I'm late," he said as he pulled on thin gloves. "I had to make a call."

"What...?"

"That's Daniel Radisson," he said, nodding at the dead man. "His friend Michael Bornstein is outside. They were going to kill you. And her."

"Why haven't you freed me?"

"I need you to hear a few things first," Blasingame said. "I need you to listen very closely and there's not a lot of time."

Ellen took a breath. "All right."

"They were supposed to be retrieving something. What they planned on doing was stealing it and cashing it in through a man in San Diego. What Daniel didn't know is that his good friend Michael had made a separate deal with San Diego to take it for himself and cut Daniel out."

"A fence?"

Blasingame nodded. "The fence betrayed them to the man they were supposed to be working for, just as he was prepared to betray Daniel for Michael. He also betrayed everyone to your friend, the FBI agent." He shook his head. "Not a man to be trusted."

"You were helping them." It was not a question.

"I told them about the Johnstons. After Brenda turned in my aunt's jewelry, San Diego told our employer what they were up to. Our employer told me to keep them from stealing what was in the case."

"He told you to kill them."

"Only if they broke the rules."

"The rules?"

"You don't steal from your employer, right, that's pretty obvious." He shook his head. "You don't kill citizens. You don't kill cops. And you sure as hell don't kill reporters. That kind of behavior lights fires. I met Michael out front. I was going to take the case from him and go away. He tried to bargain, split the case, he told me about his contact with San Diego, and promised he would make sure Brenda, Daniel, and you were dead. All the loose ends." He shrugged. "That's when I made my call."

"You killed him. I didn't hear anything."

"But here's the thing," Blasingame said, ignoring Ellen's statement. "There are rules, and there *are* exceptions to the rules. No one wants to kill a reporter, right. But the man who owns the case, he can't afford to have any of this on the front page. So the fallback position is for you and Brenda to die."

"You could do that?"

Blasingame looked at her in silence. His eyes seemed hollow, as if they were caves in which no light ever appeared. He smiled slightly and nodded.

"Believe it," he said.

"God," Ellen said. Lowering her head, she closed her eyes and for a moment felt an urge to cry. She fought it down and raised her head enough that she could see Blasingame's face. How had she so misjudged him, how had she missed what he really was? Then she remembered the thing hidden inside Blasingame, the thing that warned her off from him. She took a breath.

"To borrow an earlier question, why am I still alive?"

"That *is* the fallback," Blasingame said. He paused, letting her think about what he said. "The preferred position is, you leave me out of your story. Here's the issue. If I'm in the story, then my employer thinks there may be too many links to him and things become very complicated. If I'm not, well, then, maybe it's an unsolved mystery. These two were supposed to be retired from working for him. Everyone in New York knows it. They even had a retirement party for them. I'm sure the Albany PD had eyes and ears there. So, sure, there's that old connection to him but he thinks he can handle it. But with me, he thinks that's a link too much. What he likes is a story where two bad guys looted the dead and got killed by two other bad guys, two guys operating as independent thieves. Great story, lots of justice. Otherwise, fallback position."

"Then who killed these two?"

"I don't suppose you'd say that you did?" Blasingame smiled. "You've kind of got a rep…"

"No."

"I didn't think so. Well, Michael, badly wounded from an argument with Daniel, came in here and killed Daniel. Then Michael died trying to get away. He got as far as his car before collapsing. Even more justice. Maybe they'll make a movie. How does that work?"

"They killed each other?"

"Kind of ironic, given that Michael planned to kill Daniel at some point before leaving here anyway, or so he said. This," he held up the gun, "is his. I'll leave it beside him when I leave."

"But, Michael…"

"Died from a stab wound. Everyone will be surprised that he was able to get off the ground, come in here, and shoot Daniel, but sometimes the human spirit can't be denied."

"And Brenda and I?"

"Brenda is out, unconscious. And you want to get her an ambulance when you get free. She's been unconscious a pretty long time. You're the witness to their mutual annihilation. You were here with a gun in your face. Michael shot Daniel and left, staggering. It took you a few minutes to free yourself. You called for help." He paused. "You know the truth; all you have to do is not tell all of it. And give me your word you will remain silent about my part."

"How do you know I'll keep my word?"

"No one likes loose ends. I'd probably be one myself if you go back on your word." He paused. "Daniel and Michael broke their word to their employer and tried to cross a line. But if the two of them are just independent operators and you weren't told about their plans and who they work for, and, most especially, if I was never here, then there are no loose ends."

"What about the thing? The thing in the case?"

"What thing? Did you see anything?"

"No, but Brenda helped them find it."

"It was locked, she never saw inside it. She saw the case, sure. But never looked inside. It's out there, in the rain. Still locked. She didn't have a key, neither did they. I did. Tragedy, all this over nothing at all."

"It's not my story."

"I know. You're on vacation."

"Who *are* you?"

"Robert Blasingame. We're getting tight on time and Brenda needs help. What's your decision?"

Ellen took a breath.

"All right, you have my word. Some things need to stay hidden. All right."

"Thank you." Blasingame walked forward and picked up something from the floor. "They didn't search you, they didn't find this," he said, reaching behind her and putting the multi-tool in her hand. "But cut yourself loose so it looks right if anyone wants to study things."

He stood back.

"I have to do a little stage management. I'll be right back." He turned and left.

Ellen worked the small knife blade out of the handle of the multi-tool and sawed at the tape around her wrists. It was awkward, but the blade was extremely sharp and her hands were freed before Blasingame returned.

She had just finished with the tape holding her to the chair when he walked in. He used a bizarrely colored energy drink bottle to splash a trail of red drops behind him. Blood, she realized. He put the empty bottle in his jacket pocket. As she stood, Ellen saw there was a black knife in his other hand.

Blasingame crouched over the one she knew as Daniel Radisson and she saw him press the grip into the dead man's hand. He stood up.

"Raid, mud, the fight, no one would be surprised if there were no fingerprints at all, but there's no point in being careless." He looked at Brenda and then back at Ellen. "Get her an ambulance. It's not good that she hasn't awakened yet." He paused. "Take care of yourself, Ellen," he said and turned and walked across the kitchen.

Enough. The word came into her mind and was like a trigger.

Ellen dropped to one knee and then stood, Radisson's gun in her hands. She pointed it at Blasingame's back and thumbed the safety off. Blasingame stopped at the sound and looked behind him, raising an eyebrow.

160

"I thought we had an agreement." He raised his hands; one still held the knife.

"It was coerced," she said. "Unfair advantage."

"So, it's back to loose ends?"

"No," Ellen said. "I don't like being coerced. I don't like agreeing to something because there's a gun at my head."

"I can empathize with that, at least at the moment." He was smiling, though his hands stayed up.

"Don't be a smart ass. One option you didn't look at was I shoot you where you stand and take my chances with any fall-out from your employer. You said something about my rep."

For a heartbeat, Blasingame was silent but his smile faded and Ellen wondered if she had said too much, had pushed him into taking some kind of action.

Blasingame started to say something but Ellen interrupted.

"I'm not doing that." She lowered the gun and pushed the safety on. "I have a proposal."

"Go ahead."

"I didn't see you here. You leave. You leave Pennsylvania. I don't speak or write about you."

"Sounds like our earlier agreement."

"This time it's *my* choice." She took a deep breath. "And you leave. Now."

"I think I understand." He nodded as his hands came down. "I agree."

"All right, we have an agreement. Like I said, I can live with a few hidden things."

Blasingame turned, looked at her and smiled. He shook his head and then he was gone.

Ellen looked at the gun for a heartbeat. It seemed very heavy, as if it had gained weight as Blasingame left. She had a thought about wiping it clean of her fingerprints but she realized that wasn't needed. The police would understand why she had picked it up. She put the gun back on the floor.

She felt Brenda's pulse, and then walked to the kitchen counter and picked up the phone. She dialed 911.

"My name is Ellen Parker. I am at the residence of Brenda Cassidy. She's had a pair of intruders, burglars, I think. They killed one another. Brenda has been hurt, blow to the head. No, she's not responsive but her pulse is steady and strong. She's unconscious and tied to a chair. I'm going to free her. Yes, I'll keep the line open."

She put the phone on the counter and turned to cut Brenda free.

Evening and the days after

Chapter 6

It was several hours before Ellen returned to Willow Bed and Breakfast. Police from different agencies took the time to ask mostly the same questions, something that went on even as she stood, dried blood spattered across her clothes and hair, in the hospital corridor waiting for information on Brenda.

Karen Deevers arrived at the same time a nurse emerged to tell her Brenda was conscious. They let her talk to Brenda for only a few minutes but the police faded into the background; Ellen thought it had more to do with the arrival of Karen and her FBI windbreaker than compassion about letting her have time with the other survivor.

"Are you all right?" was the first of two questions Karen had for her but Ellen told the story again. Like the version she had told the police, she left out Blasingame. Karen let her talk. From time to time she shook her head.

"I thought the next targets would be local people Fred worked with. And I thought Carl might have built some hiding places into the garage or their homes. It didn't occur to me that the same reasoning might apply to someone who was his 'ex.' I am really, really sorry for that."

"Not your fault. You have to go with what you know."

Then Karen asked the second question.

"Why didn't you let anyone know that you thought Cassidy might be a target?"

"Dead phone," Ellen said. She took her phone from her pocked and hit its power button. The screen flashed to life and she felt her heart sink. Then it announced that it needed to be recharged and shut itself down.

"A reporter who forgot her charger." Karen shook her head.

"Hey. I'm on vacation. I'm entitled." She tried to smile.

"We have the case. Did they tell you? There's nothing in it."

"There's nothing in it?"

"You don't sound surprised. No, nothing. It could have held almost anything."

"It's been a long, long day. At this point, nothing would surprise me."

"How's Brenda?"

"She has a concussion, but they think she's going to be all right."

"You almost got her out of there. Nice try."

"They told you about that?"

"Kind of thing I'd expect you to do."

"One of these days I'll show you the big red 'S' on my chest."

"No, you're not Supergirl. What I meant was, you always try to do the right thing."

Ellen said nothing for a moment. Then she looked at her friend. "I hope you're right about that."

When she returned to Willow, she stood under her shower washing the blood and maybe everything else off until the hot water faded. Then she dressed in clean clothes. The ones stained with Radisson's blood she tied in a bundle and then put beside the cabin's trash can.

It stopped raining at some point – she hadn't noticed – and she walked to the big cabin, passing Blasingame's dark cabin. She did not bother to look at it.

There were several people there she did not recognize but Thomas and Steve sat at a small table. They looked up as she approached.

"Hey," Thomas said. "Did you have a good day?"

She laughed and then she cried. Thomas and Steve took her out of the cabin while the strangers stared. They sat in the chairs at the end of the porch. Ellen said nothing as she wiped her eyes.

"I guess you got the word after all," Steve said.

"The word?"

"Blasingame checked out. Had to return to New York, he said." He paused as he looked at her face. "I thought maybe that was what…"

"No, that wasn't it," Ellen said. She raised an eyebrow. "You thought he and I...?"

"He's terrible," Thomas said, "on the whole hetero thing. Pay him no mind. But are you all right?"

"I think so. I guess you guys haven't seen the news." They shook their heads.

Ellen told the two men an abbreviated version of what happened at Brenda's. Again, she did not mention Blasingame – she kept to the agreement.

"Brenda's in the hospital. I'm going to go over tomorrow. Probably have to wade through some police with more questions."

"Holy crap," Steve said. "That's incredible. And you're all right?"

"She's all right," Thomas said calmly before Ellen could reply. "Look at her."

"I don't know if I am," Ellen said. "Maybe I'm just good at hiding things."

The woman at the Motel Six near Harrisburg International Airport got an early start for her long drive back to Albany. She opened the door to her car and then stopped, looked up at the rooms used by the FBI to watch her, and waved goodbye. Grinning, she got into her car and drove away. One of the agents watching her through the drawn curtains sighed and wiggled a farewell with his fingers.

The fine arts fence in San Diego, confidential informant to the FBI, betrayer of Mr. Fredericks, Radisson and Bornstein, and probably others, surfaced, literally, weeks later in the San Diego Bay National Wildlife Refuge after the rope holding him to a pair of cinderblocks parted. Local police were not sure who might have attached the rope to him in the first place, inasmuch the list of suspects was relatively long. It was several months before they determined a local person took the action as a favor to Mr. Fredericks; it was a somewhat unusual method of networking but was otherwise in keeping with business principles and practices.

Kelly shared the shelf sketches from Michael Klemmer with Ellen and she agreed to having them built. A week later, he accompanied the shelves and the desk to her home and spent an afternoon taking pictures of the desk, the desk with the shelves, Ellen with the desk, Ellen using her laptop on the desk, the laptop on the desk, and came away impressed with Ellen's patience. His article was published six months later. He never told Klemmer who the shelves were for but Ellen's check did. Klemmer smiled at the gesture and called her one evening, just touching base.

Patti and Joyce continued to run Willow and it built a steady clientele doing repeat business. Breakfasts continued to be outrageous in size. Patti's brother came home from Afghanistan – everyone thought it was Afghanistan but he never said; some things need to be hidden. It was his fifth or sixth tour, Patti wasn't sure, and he and his wife spent a long weekend at Willow. He loved the breakfasts.

Karen Deevers continued to share with her friend Jack from the Albany FBI office the thought, feeling, and hunch, that Fredericks' killer had been in Coalville; it grew as she counted bodies. A tire on Radisson and Bornstein's

SUV matched the print found near Carl Johnston's body. While not doubting Ellen's account, Karen wondered if there had been someone else at Brenda's house, someone who left with whatever the case hid, someone who somehow got the two men to take each other out. But she could never find enough dots to connect and the killer, if he was ever in Coalville, remained "spooky clean."

Brenda Cassidy recovered and became the newest member of the Shot to Hell Club. Brenda did go to Delaware County Community College as planned and bolstered her academic credentials. But she found herself studying social work rather than nursing at Penn State. She thought it had something to do with finding her own way.

Robert Blasingame's reputation as a contractor and restorer grew and he became the first choice of people facing what appeared to be difficult problems of several kinds in the Albany area. When the Capital District Fraternal Order of Police (Lodge 14, Albany) were given a building of their own, Blasingame provided his time as a contractor pro bono. During an interview for a local television station, he remarked, "It's important for everyone to find a way to support law and order; it can't be a job just for the police."

Daryl Jennings' name appeared over the print and online columns reporting the killings near Coalville, which he really liked but he made a point of not celebrating his satisfaction. Some things, he remembered hearing someone say, were better kept hidden.

Steve and Thomas went home from Willow Bed and Breakfast. Four months later, they married. Ellen came; without quite realizing it, the three had formed a friendship. Steve's brothers came to the ceremony and so did Thomas' mother, but the rest of their relatives, though invited, did not, which brought just a touch of sadness to the joy of the day. They did not regret their decision. Some things, they decided, were better not hidden.

Excerpt from *Child in the Dark* by Steven M. Silver

Prelude: Sunday afternoon

Home of John Allen Douglas

Sometime during a quiet Sunday afternoon, Nicole Douglas disappeared from her very large home on Monk Road in Gladwyne, a suburb of Philadelphia. Nichole was a few days older than nine years on Sunday.

She was the daughter of Joan Ferris Douglas; more significantly, she was the step-child of John Allen Douglas. It was he who picked up the house phone – the elderly couple who maintained the house had the day off and his wife, Joan, was attending a social function that John Douglas reflexively described as "boring as shit."

The electronically-disguised voice on the phone quickly explained Nicole was in the hands of people Douglas did not know, she was alive and well, and Douglas ought to avoid talking to the police as that would result in his step-daughter being dumped into the Schuylkill River. He was told that their demands would be made the next day.

John Douglas said little besides acknowledging he understood the instructions. After the connection was broken, he hung up, went into his study and retrieved a Glock 21 9mm pistol from his wall safe and ran down the hall to Nicole's bedroom. She was not there.

"Fuck," he whispered.

It was a little after eight when his wife returned home. He told her what happened and, as he expected she would, Joan was hysterical, running first to Nicole's bedroom and then to most of the other rooms in their very large home. Douglas made no effort to keep up with her nor did he try to calm her down. He knew the former was pointless, having carefully checked the entire house himself, and the latter would just result in him becoming angry with her and probably slapping her around a little, something that was, at the moment, a luxury.

Neither got any sleep that night. On Monday, the elderly couple overseeing the house and grounds, Peter and Mary Martinez, emerged from their apartment over the converted carriage house behind the main house and set about their various tasks for the day. This included Mary briefing the part-time gardener on what Joan wanted done that week and accompanying the house cook on her shopping trip. For Peter, the morning began with freezing in complete fear when walking through the study's open door and seeing John Douglas sitting at his desk.

It was not sight of the handgun that clutched his heart. It was entirely the appearance of John Allen Douglas, his employer. His face made the Glock insignificant. Martinez had never seen a face so full of cold, focused hate. As Douglas' eyes turned on him, Martinez felt like his life was being sucked out of him.

Then Douglas blinked and his face was... Blank. Everything, hidden, but the room was so still that inhaling the air was like trying to breath in tasteless syrup.

"Peter," Douglas said, "we have a problem."

Martinez wanted to weep, for everything he knew about his employer led him to believe that whatever the problem was, it would be solved by blood.

At nine, the phone in Douglas' study rang. Though he had been without sleep for 24 hours, he listened carefully to the electronically-distorted voice and responded to the speaker's statements with no emotion. He was assured his step-daughter was alive and healthy. He asked for a proof of the truth of the statement and was told it would be provided in the next call. He was told to gather half a million dollars in unmarked bills and given 48 hours to accomplish the task. He was told not to contact the police or Nicole would be returned to him in parts. He agreed to everything the voice said.

After the caller hung up, Douglas had his wife come to the study. Exhaustion had helped calm her. In the absolute minimum of words, he described the call. Then he played back the caller's voice. His wife seemed to summon strength from deep inside her and, though her lips were almost violently pressed together, she listened to the voice. She shook her head and said she could not identify it.

Douglas could not identify the speaker either but had hoped she might have picked up something from the spacing of words, perhaps even their choice, but he knew it was a very thin reed to grasp.

He assured her that he would comply with the caller's demands, which seemed to reassure her. He did not mention he had much more than the ransom amount in another safe in the house's basement.

Then Douglas made calls of his own. The first was to David Rourke, a former extortionist, former thief, and currently working part-time for John Allen Douglas.

Rourke hurried to Douglas' home while Douglas made additional calls. The people he talked with were shocked by the news of the kidnapping, and they were people not easily shocked. Douglas had just hung up when Rourke arrived.

Rourke was an older man with thinning white hair, a slight scar on one cheek that tended to be hidden when he smiled, and was suspected in the deaths of two of Douglas' rivals for criminal power. Of the many people who worked for Douglas, he was one of the few selected by Douglas to perform tasks involving his personal and home security.

Douglas played the recording of the caller and Rourke leaned over the desk and listened silently. Twice he backed the play-back up to hear again a particular phrase.

"I think," Douglas said, "he garbled his voice because it is someone I would recognize."

Rourke nodded, thinking, and sat in chair next to the desk.

"Possible. But it might be someone your wife knows. Or someone who is just being very careful."

"Sunday, late afternoon."

"Your wife was going to the fund-raiser."

"She went."

"The Martinez couple had the day off."

"Peter says they saw nothing."

"I'm only here Monday through Friday."

"You're thinking it was someone who knew us well enough to know I'd be home alone on Sunday."

"Probably in the garage, right? Doing your hobby."

"Working on the T-bird, right. No secret, I like doing it."

"Not a secret, but the garage is on the same side as the Martinez' carriage house. Blind to her side of the house from there. Did you see her?"

170

"We had lunch together, the three of us. Joan took off at one. Nicole was doing some kind of thing for school. I went by her room around three. She was fooling around with her computer. Looking at pictures of Indians."

"India Indians or the other kind?"

"What the fuck difference does it make? God damned Sitting Bull."

"She say anything?"

"She never says much, you know that. Not to me."

"Seem nervous at all?"

"No. Barely looked up when I stuck my head in. Not a big talker."

"When did you notice she was gone, what time was it?"

"A call came in at five. I didn't have the recorder on. They said they had her. Same disguised voice. Told me they'd call later today."

"This is three kinds of bullshit." He shook his head. "I don't think this is a regular kidnapping. People know you, know of you. They have to know that there's no future in messing with your family."

"I've had much the same thought. It's about someone wanting to mess with *me*."

"Anyone been pushing at you?"

"Not since Francona. That was four, five months ago. Everyone was happy to divide his stuff up. No one griped at how things were settled."

"I haven't heard anything but I'm pretty much out of the loop nowadays. But say it is someone, someone who wants to be a rival. They've kept everything very low profile so you haven't been suspicious. They pull this shit, get you distracted, and in the middle of it all, when things get really bad, then they make a move."

"That makes a lot of sense."

"They were at least watching. They knew the Martinez' schedule, knew I wasn't here to drive her to school and home, cook and gardener off for the weekend, knew you were alone. They probably watched you working on your car while a couple of them grabbed her. That makes three people at least."

"I'm making calls. After I called you, I got in touch with Barber and then Iacono."

"Barber's a pretty steady ally of yours."

"Iacono?"

Rourke rocked his hand.

"Yeah," Douglas said, "but he's pretty old school. Big on negotiation, smoothing ruffled feathers. He wants order."

"Nothing orderly about kidnapping children. See if he mobilizes some help. What did he say?"

"He was going to check around."

"Well, Iacono does know everyone. What about Barber?"

"Same. He wondered if it was something like what we were talking about. Iacono's older, got grandkids. I think he was angry that anyone would do this kind of thing."

"Yeah, if someone's playing by new rules, then everything could get real ugly." He shook his head. "All the political bullshit to one side, we've got to get your little girl back."

"And then we've got to cut some balls off."

"Agreed."

Hidden Things cover by Eric Strehl
Blackheart Studios, http://www.ejstrehl.com

Also by Steven M. Silver

With Susan Rogers, Ph.D. *Light in the heart of darkness: EMDR and the treatment of war and terrorism survivors.*

Poetry

American Travelers
Hot Chrome, Smooth Leather, and a Red Bandanna
Victor Echo Zero Five

Fiction

The Wild Geese Saga
Mercenary's Heart
Mercenary's Honor
Mercenary's Code
Mercenary's Logic
Mercenary's Destiny
Mercenary's Soldiers
Mercenary's Redemption
Mercenary's Courage
Mercenary's Peace
Mercenary's Justice
Mercenary's Humanity
Mercenary's Promise

The Ellen Parker Series
A Dangerous Man
Killers
Woman on the Wire
Hidden Things
Child in the Dark